LOVE OF THREE

MOUNT ROXBY SERIES: BOOK FOUR

AIMIE JENNISON

LOVE OF THREE: A MOUNT ROXBY NOVELLA

MOUNT ROXBY SERIES: BOOK FOUR

AIMIE JENNISON

CONTENTS

A NOTE FOR THE READER

This book has been written using UK English and is set in Australia. I apologise if there are words or phrases you do not understand. Please feel free to contact me for further explanation, or to discuss the meaning of a particular phrase or word, via my email me at aimiejennison@gmail.com.

DEDICATION

Sometimes it's okay to love more than one person.

1.
NEVER UNDERESTIMATE A WITCH

MISTY

*C*learing the tables at the end of the night can be therapeutic—all the mess disappearing and the bar being ready for opening up the next day. Unfortunately, there are times when it isn't so good. Like tonight, when that last customer hangs around, moving with every table you clear.

I place the chairs upside down on the last table and glance around the room to make sure I haven't missed anything. All the tables leading to the dance floor are clean, and the chairs are upside down how I like them. The row of booths along the right-hand wall all have chairs upside down on the edges of the table so people know they're no longer to be used.

I turn to the bar with my cloth, preparing for my last job of the night. Well, that and nonchalantly getting the vampire who's leaning against the bar to leave.

"Look, buddy, it's time for ya to go home." I collect a handful of glasses along the bar, taking them around the other side to put them in the little dishwasher. "I wanna get home before the sun rises and I'm pretty sure you do too," I state, making it clear I know exactly what he is. I don't share his reasons for getting home before sunrise, though. I'm a witch, not a vampire.

In a flash, he's behind the bar and crowding my space.

"We could have a pretty good time between now and sunrise." He glances around the room. "Besides, it's not like this place has any windows. We could keep going until the sun puts me to sleep."

I shudder at the thought of being stuck with his lifeless body. I take a step back, and he follows. "Look, ya need to get outta my space or I won't be held responsible for my actions."

He throws his head back and lets out a heavy laugh. These other supes always underestimate us witches. Vampires and shifters are the worst culprits. Demons seem to be the only ones who remember how dangerous we can be. "You won't be held respon—"

I cut his sentence short by throwing a spell at him with a clench of my fist. He drops his head into his hand as I squeeze his brain in my fist.

"Shiit," he groans. The pain is clearly too much for him to handle.

The front door opens, and I glance that way as I step around the bar and away from the vampire.

"Is everything all right in here?" Billy, one of the local werewolves, asks from the doorway, his eyes flicking from me to the vamp.

I loosen my fist, effectively releasing my grip on the vamp's brain, but only enough for him to hear my words through the pain.

"Would ya mind giving Dominick a call?" The vamp whimpers at his king's name. "Let him know we've got a misbehaving vamp for him to pick up."

By the time I've finished my sentence, Billy already has his phone out and up to his ear. He takes a couple of seconds to relay my message before hanging up and sliding the phone into his back pocket.

"There are a couple of wolves outside who I'm going to

send home. Then I'll show Dominick in when he arrives. Are you okay with him?" He nods towards the vampire who's still holding his head in his hands.

I wipe my nose with the back of my hand and see the blood as I lift my arm away. Magic always takes a toll, and it usually demands payment in blood or power.

"We'll be fine." I give my wrist a sudden flick, effectively breaking the vamp's neck.

The vampire's body slumps to the floor and Billy gives me an appraising look. "Jesus, sugar." He clears his throat. "I need to get some air before I do something to embarrass myself," he says, walking back out the door. I catch sight of him adjusting himself in his pants before the door closes and I realise what he meant with his parting words. Could seeing me snapping a neck really have turned him on? Werewolves are known for being violent. I guess that could float his boat.

I step over the vamp as I go about cleaning the bar. He isn't dead, just incapacitated until his body heals. I'm sure Dominick will be here to deal with him long before he comes to.

There are only a couple of ways to kill a vampire: staking and beheading. Not everyone knows that there are a few other tricks, like the one I just shared with Billy. Dominick will probably be pissed at me for that, but I'll deal with those consequences later.

I slam the dishwasher closed and stand up to find Billy and Dominick strolling in the front door. They're polar opposites. Dominick is tall, dark, and handsome, always impeccable in a suit with his wiry frame and dark curls hanging around his face, whereas Billy looks rough and dangerous in his jeans and biker leathers, with his shaved head and large muscular body.

I shake my head as I rake my eyes over their bodies, trying to kill the thoughts of having them in my bed. *Jesus!*

I'd sworn I would never date another supernatural creature. Not after my ex. He was an angel, except he acted more like a demon. He was so controlling and, after seeing how the werewolves act around their mates, I can only imagine Billy would be the same, not to mention Dominick; he likes to control anything that breathes in his territory. The alpha of the Mount Roxby pack, Theo, has had to push for equal pegging in their joint ownership of the area.

"Like something you see?" Billy smirks, catching me ogling.

Dominick straightens the cuffs of his jacket. "She was clearly looking at me. This suit is fitted to perfection, after all."

I roll my eyes. "I was deciding, if I took ya both to bed with me, who'd bottom for who?" I say with a smirk. It wasn't exactly a lie. The question *had* crossed my mind when I pictured them naked in my bed.

It's well known that Dominick doesn't care about gender when he chooses his lovers. His ex-boyfriend, JD, recently turned up and caused havoc in the town. Not only did his actions make Dominick sire the alpha's sister, turning her into a vampire, but JD also murdered Theo's beta wolf, his second. JD did it all as a punishment because Dominick wouldn't make him a vampire, so I'm not surprised to see Dominick step aside and give Billy a thorough eyeing from head to foot.

"I don't bottom for anyone, but I'd definitely be happy to…" He raises a brow and a smirk crosses his face. "…*wrestle* with him over the position."

Billy steps up close so their chests are touching. "For me you will." He places a kiss on Dominick's lips, biting his bottom lip between his teeth before pulling away. "And you'll be begging to do it again." My mouth goes dry at the sight before me. *Holy shit.* I blink, unable to believe what I'm seeing.

The groans of the vamp at my feet break the heated moment.

"Bitch!" he calls as he grips my ankles, digging his nails in and drawing blood. His fangs descend at the smell of my blood, but I don't worry about him trying to feed from me. My wards won't allow such severe violence in the building. Well, unless I'm the one inflicting the violence. Dominick suddenly appears on this side of the bar, dragging the vampire up by his throat. He apparently doesn't care about the pain my wards are causing him. I throw out a hand and mutter a few words, disabling them.

"That wasn't necessary, but thank you." He walks around the bar, pausing as he reaches the door. "This—" He points his finger between Billy, me, and back to himself. "—we'll deal with this another night when the sun isn't so close to rising." He smiles. "I have a feeling we'll need plenty of time to explore things thoroughly." He disappears out the door, and I struggle to tear my eyes away from the purple painted wood.

Billy clears his throat and I watch him lock the door. "Well, that was... interesting."

I laugh. "That's not the word I'd use to describe it." I take a deep, calming breath and pull my shoulder-length hair back into a loose ponytail with an elastic band I always keep around my wrist. "Jesus, I never would've guessed ya swung that way. It was just a fantasy that popped into my head, and I couldn't keep my damn mouth shut," I say while walking around the bar and straightening the stools.

I feel Billy step up behind me. "Have I ever told you how much I like your British accent?" Placing a hand on my hip, he spins me around before sliding his other hand over my shoulder and around my neck. I grip his biceps and shake my head. "Dominick intrigues me. Someone needs to take his control away, and I wouldn't mind that being me."

He crushes his lips against mine, as if he's trying to prove he doesn't only like guys. "I'd certainly swing for you, sugar," he says, pulling back and brushing his lips against mine before capturing them in another kiss. Ignoring my rule of not dating supernatural creatures, I slide my hands up his arms and around his neck. A faint hope that my rule breaking doesn't bite me in the arse later flits around my mind, as I lose myself in the moment.

2.

BEAUTY SLEEP

BILLY

The hint of blue and purple glistens in Misty's raven-coloured hair as the rising sun shines through the open window. I've had my eye on her for a while now. I've just never had the courage to make a move, which sounds absolutely ridiculous coming from a big brute like me. The loss of our beta and the pain his mate is going through is what pushed me to make a move last night. Life is too short, and even though Alyssa is pained by the loss of Wes, I'd much rather have felt that love and lost it than never have experienced it in the first place.

I lift a strand of her raven hair and run it through my fingers. "Now, tell me more about these fantasies of yours."

She lifts herself on her elbow to look up at me, pausing the patterns her finger was drawing through my sprinkling of chest hair. "It's only like I said back at the bar. Seeing ya both walk in together… I couldn't help but imagine ya both 'ere, in bed with me. Rough and impeccable." She ducks her head, and judging by the blush floating up her cheeks, she's embarrassed by her words.

"I don't need to ask who is who," I say with a chuckle before sobering when she still won't lift her face. I lift her chin so I can see her eyes. "Why are you hiding from me?"

"I feel like a slut wanting two guys." She drops her gaze to my chest but not before I see the shame.

I kiss her forehead. "You've nothing to be ashamed of." I drop a kiss on the tip of her nose. "Hell, I'm totally turned on by the idea, and I'm pretty sure Dominick feels the same if his parting words are anything to go by." Her eyes lift to meet mine and I brush a loose hair behind her ear.

"But what will other people think?" She bites her lip with worry.

"Fuck what anyone else thinks. It's none of their business." I work her lip out from between her teeth with the edge of my thumb before placing a gentle kiss on her lips.

She lets out a jaw-cracking yawn, which makes me look at the clock. It's eight in the morning. "Jesus, I think I've kept you up long enough. You need sleep before you have to open up again this afternoon." I make a move to leave, only to find Misty's small hands pushing my chest back down.

"Stay?" she asks, giving me a pleading look. "Unless you need to be somewhere."

It's Sunday, and I have no plans for the day except a meeting with Theo later. Then I'll probably head to Misty's again like last night—the bar, not her apartment (although I won't say no if it's offered). "Let's get comfy, then. I need my beauty sleep."

Her mouth descends on mine, and I start to wonder whether she'll have the energy for another round when she pulls away. "Don't even think about it. Beauty sleep. We both need it," she says, obviously feeling my arousal against her body. Ignoring my groan, she turns on her side and settles into the crook of my arm. I cocoon her in my arms as a feeling of rightness settles within me. Last night was meant to happen. *We* were meant to happen.

After a moment of staring at the bright room, I clear my throat. "I'm sorry to be a pain in the arse, but I've gotta move, sugar. I need to shut the blinds. I can't sleep with the sun shining in my face."

She lets out a grunt before waving her arm in the air and mumbling what I can only guess is an incantation. Within seconds, the blinds close, followed by the blackout curtains, plunging us into darkness.

"That's pretty cool. We'll have to discuss what else you can do with a wave of your hands." She lifts her face enough for me to catch the glare she's giving me through tired eyes. "Later. We'll talk about that later."

I drop a kiss on the top of her head as she settles back down, and I listen to the sound of her breathing evening out, telling me she's drifted off to sleep. Only then do I close my own eyes.

Mate. My beast echoes the word through my head— the same word he released when I'd kissed Dominick earlier. I run my hand over Misty's back, feeling the tell-tale mate energy tingling under my fingertips.

They're both going to be our mate; I just need to talk them into it.

3.

DEEPEST OF SLEEPS

MISTY

*B*illy left me in bed at noon. I managed to hold onto consciousness long enough to hear him mutter something about a pack meeting and seeing me later. I think I felt him place a gentle kiss on my forehead, although that could have just been a dream.

Waking up from a deep sleep, I find myself more relaxed than I've felt in a long time. Who would have though a night with Billy could have such a good effect on me. It makes me think I should have broken my "no dating supes" rule a long time ago.

Glancing at my watch, I notice my alarm will be going off in ten minutes. With a sigh, I kick off the covers and slide out of bed. It's time to get ready for work.

I step out into the late afternoon sun and close my eyes, enjoying the heat against my skin. I wish I'd woken earlier so I could have soaked in some rays on the rooftop while grabbing my extremely late breakfast, before looking at my parking space.

My *empty* parking space. *Dammit.*

I remember that Billy had given me a lift back on his bike

last night. I guess Misty's will just have to open late tonight. I'm not worried about my customers going elsewhere for their drinks. They like to be around their own kind, and don't have to hide what they are in my place.

Humans don't know about the supernatural creatures; it keeps everyone safe that way. There are some humans who know, like the bounty hunters, also known as cleaners. They hunt supernatural creatures down and slaughter them, not caring whether they are male or female, adult or child. Most supernatural creatures are harmless to humans and choose to live harmoniously alongside them, but the cleaners don't care about that either.

The walk to the bar isn't long. I only drive so I don't have to walk the streets in the middle of the night. There are plenty of dangers for a person walking the streets at two or three in the morning, even a person with powers like mine. Anyone can be caught off guard, except maybe a werewolf like Billy. He can sense people much better than a witch can.

Billy.

I can't believe I slept with Billy last night. I'd been eyeing him up for months, but he'd never really shown an interest in me, or anyone for that matter, so I never imagined he'd reciprocate, especially after I mentioned that stuff between him and Dominick. I was certain talks of a threesome with a vampire would scare him off completely, even if he was slightly interested in me in the first place. It's common knowledge in the supernatural world that vampires and werewolves are mortal enemies. Apparently, werewolf blood is much tastier than human's, and werewolves don't like the idea of being food. I don't really blame them. After all, I don't like the idea of being a vampire snack either.

Feeling the magic of my wards pressing against my skin as I get closer to the bar distracts me. A human would feel the need to cross the road and escape the feeling as quickly as possible. If they don't, they wouldn't be able to walk over the threshold without their hearts giving out. Even a supernatural creature would feel on edge as they closed in on the bar. A werewolf's hackles would probably rise, and a vampire would feel on high alert. If they knew about the wards, they could easily ignore it. Out-of-towners might have an issue, but we don't often get those, especially ones who don't speak to either Theo Wilson or Dominick Drake. It's the law to ask permission to enter anyone's territory, and not many people are willing to risk their lives by entering without it.

There are three regulars waiting outside the bar when I arrive. Instead of going around the back to open up from inside like I usually do, I open up from the front door.

"Misty." Tom, an alcoholic witch, sags with relief and I try not to laugh at him. "We were starting to wonder if you weren't opening tonight."

They all step aside, giving me access to the door. I place my hands on the hard surface and channel my magic. "No, just running a little late, sorry."

I send the magic flowing through my fingertips to the bolts on the inside of the doors.

"*Aperi.*" I sense the bolts slide at my Latin command to open.

With a twist of the door handle, I turn to the customers and wave them in before pulsing more magic out and muttering another command, "*Ignis.*" The lights come on as commanded and I throw my bag under the bar. "What are ya'll having? First drinks on me since I made ya wait."

Matilda, a beautiful witch in her sixties, gives me a warm smile. "You don't have to do that, sweetie." She pulls a comb out of her bag and brushes it through her thinning silver hair.

"I'm more than happy to. So, what'll it be?" I look at them, waiting for their orders.

"I'll have a Jack on the rocks," Tom states. "Do you want me to pull down the chairs off the tables?"

I glance at him and see that he's already doing just that. "Thanks, Tom."

"I'll take a bottle of Corona, and a martini and lemonade for my beautiful wife," Jack says, as he plants a kiss on Matilda's forehead. The couple come in most nights, looking loved up, which is always nice to see.

As I go about pouring their drinks, Jack and Matilda chat about their grandkids. Apparently, their twelve-year-old granddaughter has just been accepted into an elite dance academy.

The doors open, and a number of Theo's wolves stroll in, animatedly chatting amongst themselves. One guy playfully shoves another, and they all join in laughing. I watch as the door closes, expecting it to reopen and Billy to follow them in, but it doesn't budge. I swallow my disappointment and serve the wolves with the usual smile on my face.

4.

ALLEY OF SURPRISE

DOMINICK

I have done nothing but think about the witch and wolf since I left the bar last night, and punished Simon, the vampire who had misbehaved. He will wake up chained in a coffin, unable to drink until I feel he deserves to come out. Ordinarily, he wouldn't have been reprimanded for harassing her since she'd already punished him by putting him down. He should have walked away after that, but stupidly, he chose to retaliate.

I bide my time while the sun sets. As king, I am lucky enough to rise before the sun sets. Unfortunately, I am still unable to walk in the sun so am stuck pacing the floors of the compound while I wait. Theo, the Mount Roxby pack alpha, and his wolves have a pack house where they are all welcome to stay at any given time, and I have a compound. Most of my vampires chose to stay there permanently because it's safe from sun and attack. Only Ruby, a newly sired vampire of mine, likes to stay elsewhere, but she is a little different.

Ruby was Theo's *human* sister until recently, when an ex-lover of mine decided to kill her and dump her on my doorstep. She is also now mated to a wolf of his. Who would have imagined a vampire and a werewolf could not only get on but also be mated? It means our coven and their pack are forever connected—an alliance, of sorts.

I make my way to the living area of the blood donors. We have a number of them living here, of their own free will, to keep us fed. We still hunt and feed but having them on hand means fewer deaths outside—usually due to being ravenous and accidentally draining an innocent. Feeling the sudden urge to feed, I gently knock the closed door, hoping someone is awake. Soft footsteps approach and the lock clicks before the door opens.

"Mr Drake." The young girl before me drops her eyes to the floor, aware of who I am, even though I've never laid eyes on her before. The taste of her fear in the air has my fangs descending.

I swallow and hide my fangs behind my lips for the moment, ignoring the need to feed. This girl looks too young to be here, and I'm not feeding from her. None of my vampires should be feeding from her. "How old are you?" I ask, unable to hide the growl behind my words.

Her shoulders straighten. "Sixteen," she says defiantly.

"*Sixteen!*" I shout. "Who the hell brought you here? I have rules. Sixteen is far too young to be a feeder."

"Master Dominick?" Elspeth, one of our oldest feeders at seventy-three, sounds surprised to see me, or maybe she's surprised that I'm shouting at the feeders. No matter what others may think, we treat our feeders well, and I have never raised my voice at them before.

"Is everything okay?" she asks. I'm sure she knows it isn't, but maybe she doesn't want to ask what's wrong.

I clear my throat to ensure I sound calmer than I feel. "I'd like to know who brought this young lady into the compound? She should not be feeding anyone."

"Oh." My anger rises as Elspeth lets out a little chuckle. *I don't like being laughed at.* "I think we've had a miscommunication. She points towards the young lady before me. "This is my great-granddaughter, Felicity."

"Flick. Everyone calls me Flick, Mr Drake," the girl says, giving Elspeth a loving glance. "Everyone except Grandma, that is."

I can see the resemblance in her jet-black hair and deep brown eyes. She looks more like Elspeth's grandfather, who happens to be one of my vampires, Casanova. He looks like he's in his late teens, but he's much older than that.

I take the girl's hand in mine and place a gentle kiss on it. "It's nice to meet you, Felicity." She gives me a sharp glance. "Flick," I try, testing the name on my lips.

I straighten and look back at Elspeth, who says, "She's not here to feed anyone—not yet anyway. She'll replace me when I pass, or when she's old enough, if the former happens first."

Flick's eyes well with tears as she slips her arm around her great-grandmother, giving her a gentle side hug.

"Is there perhaps some news I should be aware of?" I ask. Elspeth has been with us at the compound for a long time. She originally came when her family were young. But when her husband passed when they were in their fifties, she became a permanent fixture around here, only leaving when forced due to my rules of not feeding for long periods.

Elspeth reaches out and gives my hand a gentle squeeze. "No, I'm just getting older and I'm already having to cut down the number of feeds I supply. I'd like to have a replacement ready for when my time comes."

Relief falls over me. Lifting her hand, I place a quick kiss on it, causing her cheeks to blush. "You know you don't need to find your own replacement." I give her a knowing look. We are perfectly capable of finding our own feeders, and she knows it. "You of all people don't need to offer feeds to live here. I think you've paid your dues, Elspeth."

"He's right, El." Casanova's voice sounds out behind me.

Elspeth waves us both off. "There's still life in the old dog yet."

Seeing Casanova means the sun must be down. There are only a handful of us here that can rise before the sun sets, and he's not one of them.

Excited to finally be able to leave the compound, I turn on my heel and head towards the door. "Make sure everyone knows Flick is not here to feed on," I tell Cas, before calling over my shoulder, "Have a good evening, ladies."

---

*U*sing my teleportation ability, I materialise a street away from Misty's bar, remembering belatedly I still need to feed before heading to the bar tonight. I stand in the shadow of an alleyway as I watch a few people walking down the street. It doesn't take long to find my prey—a petite redhead who's distracted by the phone in her hand. She'll be easy to pull into the alley and use my compulsion on before she panics too much.

Three more steps and she'll be within my reach.

A solid arm clamps around my waist, pulling me into the alley. I let out a snarl as I turn on the person with all my anger—anger at myself for being too focused on making my meal quick, so I can finish what the witch suggested last night, and not noticing my attacker approaching.

Easily winning control with my vampire speed and power, I pin the culprit to the brick wall. My eyes lock onto a pair of hazel eyes—the same hazel eyes that had looked into mine before taking my mouth in a kiss last night. I drop my hold on Billy immediately. "*Jesus!* I could have killed you."

"I would have put up a fight if you got close to killing me." He suddenly has me pinned against the wall, his body pressed from chest to thigh against mine, showing me he had been holding back when he allowed me to have the upper hand.

"So I can see." I stare into his eyes and wonder why he isn't worried about me using my compulsion on him. A wave of hunger rolls over me, reminding me why I was here in the first place. "You realise you let my meal get away?"

He tilts his head to the side, offering me his neck. "Your meal just got upgraded."

I wet my lips with my tongue as I watch his pulse beat under the skin. Werewolf blood is so much more potent than human blood; it must be something to do with their wolf energy. It turns out there are some downsides to having an alliance with the local pack alpha. I shake my head and tear my eyes away. "As much as I'd love to taste you, I'm not willing to start a war. Theo and I have a deal—me and mine don't touch any of his wolves."

Billy turns to look me in the eye. "Theo doesn't own me. I'm offering you my vein, and I assure you, I'll make sure he knows it was my idea if it comes to that." He takes my mouth in a heated kiss, and I go with it, even though I still don't intend to feed from him. The taste of blood hits my mouth, and I realise the sneaky bastard has nicked his tongue on my fangs. They start to throb, but I don't allow them to fully descend.

I pull away, discreetly savouring the taste of his blood. "You did that on purpose, didn't you?"

"That depends." Billy smirks. "Did it change your mind?" Once again, he tilts his head to the side, offering me his vein.

My fangs fully descend and I answer by striking his neck. His potent blood flows over my tongue and I groan in ecstasy. Sliding a hand around the other side of his head, I cradle his neck as I slow down the pull on his vein. I don't want to drain him; he needs to be able to walk away from this. We're in an alley for Christ's sake. I remove my fangs from his neck, licking the wound clean as I wait for his wolf's healing to close it for him. I let out a chuckle against his skin as his hand slides frantically down my body and pulls on the zipper of my suddenly tightening trousers. I reach down and still his hand. "That's just the feeding talking. You don't really want this."

"I wanted *this* before you struck my neck," he states gruffly, grabbing my erection through my trousers. "And there's no way I'm walking away from here without getting some relief—unless I want to impersonate John Wayne. So, if you don't mind helping a guy out?" He nods, motioning at his own straining erection before taking my mouth with his once again.

Who am I to deny helping a guy out, especially when that guy is wrapping his big calloused fist around my erection?

I work at his belt and jeans, concentrating on not just ripping them off to get to the goods. Finally, I have his flesh in my hand and lose myself in the moment, somewhere I never imagined losing myself—in an alley with a wolf.

5.
TORTUROUS TASTINGS

I come, releasing myself into Dominick's hand with his mouth on mine and the memory of his fangs on my neck only moments ago. The feel of him pulling on my blood was the most erotic thing I've ever experienced, and I've been into some kinky shit in the past.

I used to think vampires had to glamour humans so they could feed, but Ruby filled us in on some of the things people don't generally know about vampires—like the feeders who are kept in the compound. After experiencing being fed on myself, I can definitely see why humans would volunteer to do it on a regular basis.

Dominick makes a show of tasting my flavour off his hand before throwing his head back and letting out a roar as he reaches his own climax. Dropping my head back against the brick wall behind me, I squeeze my eyes shut and force myself not to come again at the sight before me. *Fuck!* To see such a powerful man fall apart like that... all because of what I was doing to him, and the taste of my cum.

I reluctantly release my hold on his cock before we end up spending more time in this alley than is safe. Someone is bound to walk in on us, and if it's a pack member, they'll assume he's compelled me. *Fuck!* If this becomes a regular occurrence, we won't be able to keep it on the down-low—

not when we both hang around species with such keen senses of smell. Sliding my hand out of his pants, I angle it, trying not to transfer any of his cum onto them. Treating him to the same torture he just gave me, I lick my hand clean.

He lets out a groan. "You're really testing my willpower here."

"Hey, I'm just making sure you get what you gave." I give him a wink as I stick my tongue out to lick what's left of him off my lips. I'm suddenly pressed against the wall, once again with Dominick's mouth on mine.

I slide my hand into the soft curls at the base of his neck, tugging them roughly as I spin us around and slam his back against the wall. He grunts at the impact but doesn't break the kiss. When I feel like I've had my fill, I pull my mouth off his just enough to speak.

"We should really leave." I lean back enough to look in his eyes. "Maybe we could pick this up later, with a little raven-haired beauty joining in?"

He tilts his head back with a laugh. "That sounds like a wonderful idea."

As he straightens, I spot red dust in his hair and reach up to brush it out. "You've got brick in your hair." I laugh, stepping back and zipping up my jeans, giving him room to step away from the wall.

"Hmm…," Dominick says as we both survey the wall. There's a person-sized dent in the wall with cracks going in all directions. "It looks like we caused a little destruction in our moment of passion."

"*What the fuck?*" yells a voice from corner of the alley.

"Did you hear that thud?" another voice asks.

"*Hear?* I fucking felt it," the first voice replies. "I thought the wall was going to come down on me."

I glance at Dominick with wide eyes. *Shit!* It's clearly a person-shaped dent and it's not like we can explain it or bloody well disguise it. Raising a fist, I punch around the top of the shape, hoping to at least take the head and shoulder shape away. I get four punches in before Dominick pulls me back.

"It's too late. I'll deal with this." I glance at him as my back stiffens, hoping he isn't insinuating that he'll kill the people. Werewolves don't kill humans but from what I've heard of vampires, they couldn't care less if they killed someone, as long as the secret of their existence isn't threatened. "I'll use my compulsion on them. *Go!*"

Relief floods me, but guilt follows. I give him a quick peck on the lips before running deeper into the alley, taking a less public route to Misty's. Kicking a stone out of my path, I grin to myself unable to wipe the sight of Dominick in the throes of climax from my mind. He's a beautiful man but seeing him like that makes me realise there's so much more. My jeans start to tighten at the thought, and I adjust myself before I step around the corner and in through the entrance of the bar.

6.
CHAOS ENSUES

DOMINICK

*A*fter compelling the occupants of the building, making them think the damage was just a freak accident, I pull out my phone and call a local builder I know will be happy to help me out.

"Rhodes Construction."

"Bartholomew, I have a job for you if you'd like it?"

He laughs down the phone. "It doesn't matter how many times I tell you to call me Barry, does it? You'll never do it." He sighs. "Give me the address. Do I need to attend to it immediately?"

"It can be left until tomorrow," I reply, before giving him the address.

"How's my son doing? He should be due a break from your compound soon." His words make me smile. Bartholomew may like taking my money for the jobs I throw his way, but he greatly dislikes that his son is my occasional lover and feeder.

"Gerry is free to come and go as he pleases. I don't hold any of our guests captive." I force myself not to tell him he was the reason his son came to me in the first place. That's up to Gerry, not me. He's right to believe that Gerry is due a break from feeding; he's currently a week into his break. If someone feeds too often for too long, they lose themselves and become nothing more than a walking zombie feeder.

Bartholomew sighs into the phone. "If you could tell him I'd love a visit or even just a phone call. His mum misses him too."

It's my turn to sigh now. I rub a hand over my face. "I'll be sure to pass the message on."

"Thanks. I'll get on that job first thing." The call ends, and I slide my phone back in my pocket before heading to Misty's. I need a drink and some other distraction, preferably in the form of a beautiful witch and a big bad wolf.

I've been lurking in the corner of the room with a couple of my fellow vampires, including Casanova. He's always flirting with someone, so when I tear my eyes from Misty and Billy, who are chatting at the bar, I'm not at all surprised to find him flirting with a female. The fact that she's a wolf does surprise me, though.

Wolves and vampires have a love-hate relationship: we love to hate each other. Ruby mating with Eddie didn't seem unusual since she'd been brought up with the wolves before her turning. Perhaps he's only flirting to aggravate her pack mates. Hell, I can't exactly question his motives. I was in an alley with a Mount Roxby pack member not that long ago, and I plan to do it again, hopefully tonight. Theodore Wilson, the pack alpha, will be far from happy if he ever finds out.

The female wolf looks to be enjoying Casanova's attention. She throws her arms around his neck and grinds against him in time to the music. One of her pack mates separates the two, unhooking her hands and shoving himself between the wolf and the vampire. The female pushes at his back as

Casanova bares his fangs at him. Knowing Misty's wards will stop them from killing each other, I don't bother stepping forward to break things up. They can suffer the pain of the wards; it will teach them a lesson or two.

In the blink of an eye, the wolf cocks his fist back and smashes it into Casanova's face, spraying blood everywhere. After a second's hesitation, Casanova pounces on the wolf, fangs bared.

Fuck. They're going to kill each other. I stride over, pushing my way through the circle of spectators—wolves cheering the wolf on and vampires cheering for Casanova. The two are suddenly torn apart by an invisible entity and are thrown to opposites sides of the room.

Misty walks into the crowd, her hands raised. "There'll be no fighting in my goddamn bar. There will be consequences for anyone who breaks that rule." Both fighters fall to the floor, cradling their heads while screaming in agony.

I step closer to Misty as two older witches do the same, the female placing a gentle hand on her shoulder. "Misty darling, is there a problem with your ward?"

Misty shakes her head. "There was an incident last night, and I dropped the anti-violence ward. I forgot to put it back up afterwards." An angry frown forms on her face. "Bloody stupid," she mutters to herself, but anyone with supernatural can hear her.

"Let us hold those two while you reset your wards," the male witch offers.

She turns her head to look at the witches over her shoulder, never dropping her control over the two writhing on the floor. "Once the wards come back on, it'll hurt you." She shakes her head in denial. "I can't ask you to do that."

They each hold out their hands, focusing on Casanova and the wolf, as they step up beside her. "You're not asking, Misty. We're offering."

Misty's arms drop, and she takes a few steps back before closing her eyes. I watch her mouth move as she chants a spell, but I don't hear the words, even with my supernatural hearing.

Billy steps up on her left, a concerned frown on his face. Catching the scent of blood on the air, I step up to her right and glance down to see blood dripping from Misty's nose. "You're bleeding," I say, startled by the sight and worried for her wellbeing. Anyone watching and listening would most probably think my concern is towards the fact that any of my vampires in the bar would be able to scent her blood. The temptation of blood and lack of wards could easily turn this into a disaster.

"Spells always take a payment," she says through gritted teeth.

"What can we do?" Billy asks. Clearly, he's as worried as I am.

Her eyes pop open, and she glances from Billy to me, holding a hand out to each of us. "Share your energy with me and let me feed your power into the spell?"

We both take her hand without a second's hesitation.

7.

TOGETHER AT LAST

MISTY

Channelling Dominick and Billy's power, I weave it into the ward, hoping the fact that they are both high up in their supernatural hierarchies is enough for the payment. I don't feel the pain it usually causes, and I start to wonder whether it's working. I've never considered the possibility of using another supernatural being's power in my wards. Evil witches do it all the time, so it should work. Although, they take the power without permission so maybe that's what gives the spell power.

"*Crikey!*" Jack calls out as he drops his hand, rubbing it against his jean-clad thigh. "That's got some bite to it."

Matilda rubs her hands together as if she's trying to warm them. She's more likely trying to rub the pain away.

I drop the guys' hands and give them a small smile. "Thanks, guys. I would have been drained if I tried to do that on my own. Ya drinks are on me tonight." Dominick frowns and I have a feeling he wants to argue the offer, so before he can get a word out, I turn my attention towards Jack and Matilda and lead them to the bar with a firm hand on their shoulders. "Ya drinks are on me tonight, so what can I get ya?"

"You don't have to do that, Misty. We were happy to help you out," Matilda argues.

I lean over the bar and tell the girls that Matilda, Jack, Dominick, and Billy's drinks are free for the night before heading towards the toilets to clean the blood off my face. It's starting to feel crusty around my nostrils, so I can only imagine how awful it looks.

I grimace as I look at my reflection in the mirror. My deathly pale complexion and the crusty blood make me look like I've just been fighting for my life. Bracing myself by gripping the bench top, I close my eyes and drop my head as I start to wane with the loss of adrenaline.

Gentle hands pull my hair back from my face as another pair of hands tilts my chin to the side.

I open my eyes to find Dominick's black endless eyes brimming with concern. He dabs at the blood on my face with a damp paper towel. "You look drained."

"It's just the loss of adrenaline. I'll be okay in a minute."

Billy's hands drop my hair and come to rest on my shoulders. I feel myself leaning into him. "Let us take care of you."

I shake my head as I force myself to pull away from the strength and warmth of his body. "I can't close up for hours yet."

"Leave the bar in Lucy's hands. It's not like she hasn't run the place before," Dominick says. The suggestion is so strong that I daren't look at him in case he tries to use his compulsion on me. "I'd *never* use my compulsion on you."

I flick my eyes to his, shocked at how close to my thoughts he is.

"You're easy to read, princess," he says, answering the question he must have read on my face. *Are you reading my mind?*

I look at myself in the mirror and realise they may have a point. By the end of the night, I'll be in even worse shape, and I'll have no chance of recovering in time to open up tomorrow. I flick my eyes to Billy's reflection and catch him studying me with a furrowed brow. "Okay. I'll go tell Lucy, and then we can leave."

"No. I'll go speak with Lucy." I watch in the mirror as Dominick looks at Billy. "You take Misty. I'll join you shortly." Without another word, he turns on his heel and exits the bathroom.

I frown, wondering how he'll find us. He's never been to my apartment and as far as I know, he hasn't been to Billy's either. Billy lifts me into his arms and I squeal in surprise. He steps out of the bathroom and strides out of the emergency exit at the end of the corridor. After a few moments, I realise he's walking us the whole way—not heading to my apartment as I'd expected. "Where are we going?"

"My place," he states, keeping his eyes on the path ahead.

"And you're going to carry me the whole way?" I ask, feeling somewhat self-conscious of my weight and the strain it must be causing him to be carrying me for so long.

"I am. I like the feel of you in my arms." His answer makes my worries flee and I melt into his hold, enjoying being in his arms.

I open my eyes and find myself nestled into a soft mattress, a thick quilt pulled up to my chin. I must have fallen asleep on the walk over. Sliding out of bed, I head for the male voices I hear coming from another room. The timber floor below my feet is a pleasant change to my luxurious carpet. It suits Billy's style, as does the simple yet modern interior design around the room. I could spend time taking it all in, but the voices are drawing me to them.

"Dawn is fast approaching. I'll have to leave soon," I hear Dominick say as I near the door.

I pause in the doorway as the two of them come into view. Billy is sprawled back on a couch while Dominick rests his back against Billy's chest. Billy's hand is absently running through Dominick's dark curls. "You can stay. My blinds are blackout, and no one will enter without my opening the door for them."

Seeing them cuddled up together makes me feel like a third wheel. I expected to bring them together, but it looks like they're doing fine without me. Jesus, what is wrong with me? I've never been insecure in my life.

"Even in an emergency?" I call from the doorway, suddenly concerned for Dominick's wellbeing.

They both turn their heads in my direction. The broad smile that graces both their faces chases away my insecurity in an instant.

"Hey, princess."

Dominick greets me as Billy asks, "You feeling better, sugar?"

I smile as I walk towards them. "Much." I nod. "How long did I sleep?"

Billy lifts his hand from Dominick's hair to glance at his watch. "A few hours. It's almost dawn." He sighs. "And to answer your previous question, no, I can't guarantee that no one would enter in an emergency."

Dominick sits up and shuffles away from Billy, who doesn't fight to keep him there. "In that case, come join us Misty. Let us make the most of what little time we have left." He pats the space between them.

"Once we tell people about us, they'll know never to enter. Not even in an emergency," Billy says, shaking his head.

Dominick places a hand on Billy's knee. "Billy, it's fine.

We can have a little fun now, and then you two can enjoy each other's company after I leave." Dominick removes his hand as I stop before them.

I reach out and stroke my hand over Billy's head feeling the prickle of stubble under my hand. "We'll have plenty of nights to spend together when we tell 'em." He gives me a small smile, and I peck him on the lips before taking a seat between them on the sofa. I want this between the three of us to work and I have a feeling it will. I'm sure we'll have obstacles pop up, but we all seem as committed as each other and that's all that matters.

Dominick drops to his knees in front of me and pulls me forward so my arse is on the very edge. He stretches up and takes my mouth with his, kissing me passionately.

I melt into his kiss letting him take what he wants before he has to leave. Excitement rolls through me. Having never kissed a vampire before, I didn't know what to expect. Admittedly, I'd imagined his fangs would get in the way and make the kiss feel all kinds of awkward, but as his tongue expertly dances with mine, I realise I can't even feel them.

After one final stroke of his tongue against mine, he breaks the kiss. "Take over her mouth, Billy. I want to kiss elsewhere."

"With pleasure," I hear Billy reply before his face is in front of mine and he's locking lips with me like Dominick had requested. My heart beats in my chest erratically at their words. The anticipation builds as I think about where Dominick might be heading. I'm pressed back into the cushions of the couch as Dominick's deft hands strip the clothes off the lower half of my body.

Hot hands part my knees and he lets out a curse. "*Fuck!*" My need doubles at the sight of Dominick so close to where I want him. The tell-tale throbbing making it clear he'll see evidence of my need in the wetness that will be there.

Billy pulls away, and I catch him glancing down my body. "Beautiful, isn't she?"

"Exquisite."

I feel like I'm the most beautiful thing either of them has ever seen. Dominick's eyes fall on mine as he inches towards his prize. "That's right, princess. Watch me."

We keep eye contact as the heat of his mouth brushes over my most private place. The sensation of Billy pressing gentle kisses over my neck and chest as his hands pull off my top, along with Dominick's mouth working its magic, means I don't last long. My head falls back on the couch, and I close my eyes in ecstasy as Billy's wet mouth laps at the nipple he freed from my bra. As I slow my heavy breaths, Dominick kisses his way up my body, stopping at the breast not receiving Billy's attention. As I watch them locking eyes with each other as they both enjoy my body, a burst of hope runs through me. Hope for this working between us, because I've never felt anything as wonderful as this before, and I want to explore *everything* we can do together.

8

FAVOURITE PEOPLE

DOMINICK

*W*alking into the bar, my eyes immediately roam behind the counter, looking for my beautiful witch and big bad wolf, knowing he'll be within arms-reach of her if he's here. For the last couple of nights, we've spent every moment of free time we have together. And it's something I want to become a regular occurrence. My heart thuds in my chest as I finally spot them at a table of wolves, Misty sitting on Billy's lap. I never imagined I'd feel so much for two people in such a short time. It doesn't worry me; it only makes me certain that I'll do everything in my power to ensure nothing comes between us.

I straighten my suit and stride over. "Well, if it isn't my favourite people all at one table." Just opening my mouth tends to piss the alpha off, and it makes me smirk.

Theo growls, eliciting a playful smack from Bel. "Behave."

Theo sighs. "Dominick," he says, greeting me with a slight nod. I glance around the table and recognise most of the faces, but I can't place the very pregnant blonde leaning into Cain's side. The shudder that runs through her body as she glances at me makes it perfectly clear how she feels about vampires. Clearly, she's been listening to Theo. I thought his opinion of the undead would have changed after his sister joined us, but obviously not. Ruby is sitting beside Cain, Ruby and Theo's brother, with Eddie, her new mate leaning into her from the stool on her other side. He places a trail of kisses over her shoulder. I glance at Misty and continue towards them, coming to a stop behind Billy. I place my hand on his shoulder, thinking about the trail of kisses I could place there. I give it a gentle squeeze before dropping my hand. Any more attention may cause his pack to question him about it later. Seeing Cain's stiff posture tells me those questions may already be unavoidable for Billy.

"Ruby, I haven't seen you at the compound lately. Are you keeping well fed?" I ask, hoping to distract everyone.

"I was actually there yesterday, but there was no sight of you, which is somewhat strange considering you're the king and all." The curiosity in Ruby's voice seems to interest everyone around the table. Theo sits forward slightly in his seat. Bel squints at me as if she's trying to read my mind, although, she's more likely to be trying to sense my emotions since she's an empath, not a mind reader.

"I may have been otherwise engaged yesterday." I can't help but glance across at Bel, frowning under her scrutiny.

"You're seeing someone. You actually care about them," Bel accuses, sounding shocked at her own discovery.

I wave a hand dismissively. "I do have the ability to care for another person. I'm not a complete monster." I shake my head in disbelief. I thought we'd actually started to under-stand each other in the last few months. "Anyway, I do believe you wanted to ask me something, Theo?" He'd called me earlier in the day, asking if I'd be here. When I'd told him yes, he insisted I seek him out as we needed to have words. Last time we had words, it was due to his sister's change, which then led to his beta being murdered. I'm just hoping this isn't another issue like that. I don't think our alliance will survive another death.

Theo clears his throat before speaking. "Yes. Have you given permission to a fox, or a skulk of them, to enter my territory?"

"*Our* territory," I correct, somewhat irritated that he insists that I treat him as an equal when he and his pack look at me and mine as nothing but monsters. "No, the lion was the last shifter I allowed in, and I believe we agreed that you would deal with shifter requests from then on." My hands form fists at my sides as I try to dispel my sudden irritation.

"We did, but we had a fox turn up at the pack house, and I wanted to make sure they didn't have permission before I retaliated." Theo's threat of retaliation makes me smile. He's going to take this on himself, which means me and mine are not going to be dragged into it for once. Looking at the determined set of his shoulders, he's going to be as ruthless as I've heard he can be.

Out of the corner of my eye, I catch sight of Cain comforting the pregnant female by rubbing her arm. "Hey, everyone will be fine. It's what we do," he says.

Maybe this blonde beauty is his mate?

Misty jumps off Billy's knee, startling me. "Well, it's been entertaining, but my break's up. I'll try and catch ya'll later."

Taking that as my cue to leave and at least spend some time with one of my loves, I turn my attention to her. "I'll walk you back to the bar." I offer Misty the crook of my arm, but not before discreetly running a finger over the back of Billy's neck, smiling at the shiver it incites from him.

Misty takes my arm, hugging it to her body. The softness of her breasts brushing against me causes a stir below my belt. "Well, thank ya, kind sir."

"Misty! We have a lot to talk about, girl," Bel calls out as we walk away from the table; she's obviously picked up on something, and I wonder whether that will put Misty or even Billy off. I have the sudden urge to turn and plant a kiss on

Billy, wanting to make it clear he's mine and Misty's, and no one else's. It takes all the willpower I possess to not follow through with the thought. I know he has concerns about his pack's reaction and wants to speak with Theo before we make any announcements, and I even respect those wishes, but it's so difficult just walking away from him.

"Sure thing," Misty shouts, not even bothering to turn her head Bel's way, knowing Bel would hear her with her werewolf hearing no matter where she is in the bar. She squeezes my arm and I glance down at her to see her shoulders are as stiff as mine feel.

I lean down and whisper in her ear, so no one with supernatural hearing will overhear, "You don't want to leave him there either."

She flicks her eyes up to mine. "It's much harder than I expected."

Misty lets go of me, discreetly sliding her hand across the small of my back as she walks around me, before ducking behind the counter. She makes quick work of mixing a drink before placing the glass in front of me. I don't need to taste it to know it's my favourite.

"How did you know that's what I wanted?"

She gives me a disappointed look. "You've been coming in here for how long, Dominick? Do you really think I wouldn't take notice that a Siberian fizz is your favourite?"

I drop my eyes, feeling somewhat guilty about underestimating her. "I'm sorry. I didn't think you'd paid that much attention to me."

"I've had my eye on you for a long time. It was only my self-imposed 'no supe' dating rule stopping me from making a move," she admits.

I let out a relived breath. "Well, I, for one, am glad you decided to throw that rule out the window." Reaching my hand out, I entwine my fingers with hers and lift her hand to place a gentle kiss on her soft skin. I love this woman so much and wish I could come out and say it. All I can do is hope she sees it in my eyes, my actions, and hears it behind the words. When I get her home later tonight, I'll be telling her and showing her, as I will Billy too.

"I'm pretty glad about that too," she admits. Her eyes flick behind me as she drops my hand, a blush suddenly covering her cheeks.

I sense Niko and Sam before the two vampires step up beside me. Niko's arm's draped over Sam's shoulder. He presses a kiss to her temple before giving me a scrutinizing look. "Is the witch the reason you ended things with Gerry?"

I know I should tell my coven about Misty and Billy, but now is not the time. Billy wants to tell Theo first and I respect that. My coven won't have an issue with our ménage, or at least *if* they have an issue, it won't change anything. They'll get over it and learn to accept Misty and Billy as my partners, my mates. Theo is Billy's alpha and he has the power to demand Billy pick between me and the pack. The thought causes my stomach to churn because I don't really know if given that option, which he'd choose. I'd want to think it's me but knowing how close the pack is…. It's closer than family and I don't think he'd be able to walk away from that. I'm also not telling them about only half of my relationship. The three of us are a partnership; it's all or nothing.

"Can I get you two a drink?" Misty asks. I try to read her face to see what she's thinking but can't seem to pick up on anything. Part of me wishes I'd drank her blood and therefore be privy to her thoughts, like I often can with feeders, but we're not together to use each other, and the act of feeding from her isn't something I want to do right now. Billy instigated the feeding I took from him and thankfully, it didn't change anything between us. I wouldn't want it to make him feel more compliant towards me or give me the upper hand over him. So, I'm certainly not willing to risk that with Misty. I believe it was the strength of his wolf that saved him from my abilities. I'm not sure if Misty's magic would be as strong.

"We'll both have the same as him." Sam gestures to my drink, and I quickly take a mouthful, having been reminded it's there.

With the comfort of the familiar liquid leaving a trail down my throat, I turn to answer Nick's question, feeling Misty's eyes boring into me. "Things between me and Gerry needed to come to an end. I care for him, but I knew his feelings for me were getting stronger and it wasn't fair to keep him around thinking there was a chance for things to change on my end."

"So, you just broke his heart for his own good?" Niko asks, anger evident in his voice. The reaction surprises me because Niko has never shown any interest in mine and Gerry's relationship.

"Niklaus, leave Dominick alone." Sam bats his arm before turning her attention to me. "Ignore him, Dom. Gerry isn't heartbroken. I had a chat with him before he left to visit his family and whatever you said to him, he got it. To be honest, there seemed to be a weight lifted off his shoulders." She gives me a calculating look. "In fact, if I didn't know you better, I'd think you'd compelled him into being okay with it all."

Anger flows over me that the thought even crossed her mind. I would never compel anyone who I care about. It's one thing, Theo and his pack assuming I'm a monster, but my own people… my *friends*. They should know. My fists clench at my side, nails biting into my palms as my eyes roam the bar looking for something to ground me. They fall on Misty, serving someone at the other end of the counter. And as if she can feel my eyes on her, she glances at me over her shoulder. A frown forms between her brows and the concern on her face helps calm me. I take a deep breath and give her a small smile. A hand brushes over my back, and I feel Billy's energy running along my skin as he steps up beside me. One of the barmaids ask him for his order but he turns to me.

"Are you okay?" His eyes bore into mine, letting me know he sensed my anger. "Or were you next?"

"I'm good," I say, gesturing to my half-full glass, all the while thanking my lucky stars that I managed to find these two wonderful people to share my life with. I just hope they both feel the same way.

9

NOT ASKING
PERMISSION

BILLY

The weeks have passed and things between the three of us have only gotten stronger, making it harder and harder to ignore my wolf when all he wants to do is claim our mates. That is why I find myself here, lounging on the sofa, waiting for Theo to finish up with his meeting. The need to explain my relationship status to him as soon as possible since mating a vampire could affect the pack has been weighing on me for days. The last thing I want is to put anyone in danger, least of all my pack. I wish I could have talked this over with my packmates but that would mean having them keep things from the alpha, and I can't ask that of anyone. And anyway, Theo is one of my closest pack-mates, so he'd be finding out anyway. It's just right to tell him packmate to alpha, first. He deserves that respect.

Bel hands me a mug before sitting on the sofa opposite me. "Don't look so worried. He won't kick you out for mating." I look at her with wide eyes, wondering how the hell she knows. I know she's an empath but that doesn't mean she can read minds. She laughs. "Misty called before you arrived and mentioned you were coming to discuss mating some-one." I relax slightly, knowing she isn't psychic.

Last night, Dom had declared his love for us both and we'd all reciprocated. I'd told them about my need to claim them both as mates and surprisingly, neither of them batted an eyelid. In fact, they were both extremely happy about the idea. I was certain Dom would run a mile at the thought of being tied down to someone for the rest of my life, or maybe even his life. Eternity, is a long time. Usually with matings between humans and wolves, the human's aging process will be slowed to their wolf partners and they will have an extended life to live as long as their wolf mate, but with Dominick being immortal, we aren't too sure what that may mean for the three of us. Will Misty and I both live for all eternity providing we aren't killed in battle or an accident?

I sigh. "I know, but it's the *who* that's going to bother him."

Bel releases her hair from its tie, before pulling it back and securing it once again. "If he can handle Cain's mating and still have him as his beta, he'll handle your choices too."

I pause with the mug just before my mouth. "Choices?"

"I spoke to Misty, remember? I've put two and two together... and come up with three." She offers with a wink.

I laugh. "Sounds like you're on the right track. You're really sure he'll accept it?"

"Accept what?" asks Theo from the doorway.

I turn in my seat to greet him. "Theo, hey!"

He strides over and kisses Bel on the head. She stands and waves for Theo to take her seat. "I'll leave you to it." She gives my shoulder a gentle squeeze as she passes.

I rub the rim of my mug with my thumb as I try to push back my nerves. Bel is probably right; she knows Theo better than anyone. He'll handle it fine. *I hope he will anyway.*

"What's on your mind, Billy?" Theo asks, breaking into my thoughts.

I take a deep breath to centre myself before unleashing my worries. "I've found my mate." A broad smile crosses his face, and I push on before he can jump in. "But it's complicated. There are two of them." I grimace, but it's not like I'm ashamed. I just know a lot of people won't understand our situation.

"Two mates? I don't... is that even possible?" he asks, a frown etched on his face.

I run a hand over my shaved head, realising it's due for a run over with a razor. "My wolf has chosen two mates. So yes, it's possible—for me anyway."

"They're going to want to kill each other. We don't share. It's not in our nature." Theo leans forward in his seat, searching my face for God only knows what.

"They're not wolves, and we're happy together... the three of us." I give him a pointed look, hoping he understands.

He smirks as he reclines back into the sofa. I pick up my mug, downing what's left of my drink. "You're going to have a few of the guys jealous, walking around with a girl on each arm."

I sputter as I choke on my coffee. "Only one of them is a girl." My face heats and I want to kick myself for it.

Theo's face turns a deep shade of crimson, and I wonder if it's darker than my own. "I... well, I'm sorry I jumped to that conclusion." His brow crinkles.

I wait for him to ask whatever question is forming in his head.

"Did you really think I wouldn't be open-minded enough to accept you having a male and female mate?" he asks.

I shake my head. "No, it's more complicated than that. It's *who* they are that concerns me."

"So, I know them?" He runs a hand through his hair, leaving it sticking up in a mess of directions. "Well, you might as well let the cat out the bag, before it scratches its own way out and causes more damage."

I frown at his analogy and, realising I probably won't

ever get it, I shake my head to remove it from my thoughts. "Before I tell you who it is... I need you to understand I'm not here to ask permission. I'm taking these two... incredible people as my mates no matter how you feel about it. I'm here as a courtesy. If you don't like my choice in mates, I'm willing to step away from the pack, if that's what you request."

"Now you have me worried." Theo pins me with a stare, one that I can't seem to look away from.

I stand, keeping eye contact. "Do you mind...?" I gesture to the open space beside the sofas, indicating I'd like to pace. He nods, and I step into the space. "My mates are Misty and Dominick." I drop the bomb quickly and hold my breath as tension fills my body, waiting for his reaction.

"Dominick. As in Dominick Drake?" His sentence ends on a growl, and I can't help but feel the need to submit.

I drop into the chair and rub at my face, trying to remove the tingles left behind from his alpha energy against my skin. "Yes, the one and only." I sigh, knowing what's going to come next. I'll be cutting ties with the pack. There's no way Theo will allow Dominick to be tied to the pack bonds by mating with me. Just a short while ago, they were the worst of enemies. "Look, I don't want to put the pack in danger, so don't worry if you feel like you need to give me my marching orders. I'm dominant enough to be a lone wolf. You don't need to worry about my wellbeing."

Theo laughs. "I'm not worried about you. I know how strong you are." He quirks a brow. "Being mated to Dominick, the vampire king, would also be a pretty good deterrent, although that could put an equally big target on your back too."

"I know we're still unsure how Ruby and Eddie's vampire and werewolf mating bond will affect the pack. I understand how bringing Dominick into the fold will be a bigger worry." Concerned about his reply, I chew the inside of my cheek.

Theo stands, stepping over to the large glass windows to look out over the yard and surrounding forest. After waiting in silence for a number of minutes, I join him at the window. Just as I start to give up on hearing his reply, he opens his mouth. "You love him?"

"I do—more than I realised I ever could love someone, let alone two people at once." I shake my head. "It's new to us too, but one thing we are all certain of is the love." He watches me out the corner of my eye and know he's seen my mushy face as I spoke. Hell, I could feel myself practically swoon as I shared news of my mates with him. I'm a grown arse man. I like to think I'm one of the toughest, but when I talk about Dom and Misty, I can't stop myself from turning into a mushy bastard.

"I'm not kicking you out of the pack because of who you love. If your mating bond with Dominick puts the pack in danger, we'll deal with it. For now, I'm going to say congratulations." Theo pulls me into a hug, giving me a quick pat on the back before releasing me.

"Thanks, Theo." I let out a sigh of relief, and a huge weight seems to lift off my shoulders. "You don't know what a relief it is to hear you say that." I swallow down the lump in my throat as I fight away the urge to cry.

Theo laughs before waving me off. "Go! I have a feeling you've got a couple of people who need to hear a thing or two from you. Go claim your mates."

I immediately make a beeline for the door, both me and my wolf eager to do just as Theo suggested.

10.

LOVE OF THREE

MISTY

I take one last bite of my sandwich before loading my dirty plate into the dishwasher under the counter. I set it to go on a fast wash, dancing around Billy's kitchen to the country tunes playing on my phone.

We've been spending most of our spare time here since Billy's house is detached and his neighbours are less likely to hear us than mine are. Billy warned me that he was meeting with Theo this afternoon, which could make him get home a little late. I've been worried all day about how the meeting would go. I even called Bel, to try and gauge how Theo would handle the news without actually telling her everything. Dominick always turns up just after dusk, eager to be with the two of us. So, I know once he arrives, he'll be able to take my mind off my worries.

There's a pop behind me and, as if my thoughts conjured him, Dominick's hands slide around my waist. Each vampire has certain gifts, and one of Dominick's is teleportation. I turn in his arms, and we sway to the music. "Has my princess had a pleasant day?"

"Now that I'm in ya arms, yeah," I admit, not allowing myself to feel self-conscious about showing such strong feelings towards him.

His mouth falls on mine in a possessive kiss. He pulls

away a fraction, his lips still brushing mine. "I love you." My emotions skyrocket as my heart beats double time. Other than my immediate family, no one has ever told me they love me.

"You two are a sight for sore eyes," Billy calls out as he places his shoes neatly by the door. The main living area is all open plan so you can see it all from the front door. The only rooms with doors on them are the bathroom, bedrooms, and toilet. Knowing where he's just come from and what the conversation was about, I release my hold on Dominick. "Go show 'im some love, and I'll get us all a drink. We might need 'em."

Dominick heads straight for Billy, pulling him into his arms as they meet in the middle of the lounge area. "I don't care what he says, I'm not letting him cut you out of the pack. You can claim Misty, and we'll just stay as we are. I won't be hurt by that."

Billy plants a quick kiss on Dominick's mouth. "I love you," he breathes, pulling away. My heart warms at hearing those three words being said between the two of them. We'd all declared our love the night before, with Billy telling us about feeling the need to claim us as his mates. We'd made love and it was amazing. I couldn't imagine feeling any more in love but every time I hear those words afresh, my heart seems to swell even more.

"I love you, too. I can't walk away from you." He turns his head, pinning me with a stare as I place our drinks on the coffee table. "Either of you." His words cause something inside of me to settle and I know no matter what Theo said, he won't be leaving either of us.

Billy releases Dominick. "Grab a seat, Dom."

Billy gives me a hug and plants a kiss on the top of my head as he passes me. "You okay?" he asks.

I reply with a nod, not wanting to turn the subject away from the important stuff.

"You can both stop looking so worried. No one is leaving anybody, okay?" He sits on the edge of the sofa with his body turned towards Dominick. I rest on the arm of the chair beside Dominick and give Billy my full attention. "I'm not leaving the pack either." Billy's eyes are focused on Dominick as he speaks, perhaps looking for something in his reaction.

"You didn't tell him?" Dominick nods absently. "That's okay. I told you, I will not take it personally." Although Dom's words sound honest, I can hear the hurt lying behind them. It hurts my own heart and I feel the need to kiss away his pain.

Billy slides across the couch and gives Dominick a hard kiss. Seeing the kiss between them makes me relax a little. "Will you let me finish what I was saying?"

I slide my hand comfortingly over Dominick's shoulder as he turns his body towards Billy. Lifting his hand, he takes mine in his, giving it a gentle caress. "Of course."

"Theo has accepted our situation."

"No questions asked?" Dominick presses.

Billy rubs a thumb over Dominick's brow, trying to wipe away his frown. "He asked the only question that matters… do I love you?"

"Theo loves Bel fiercely. He's not gonna force Billy to choose between his love for us and love for his pack." I slide my arms around Dominick's neck, hugging him from behind. Relief and excitement courses through me, knowing that now we can all be happy together without the threat of Theo or the pack tearing us apart.

Billy kneels before us, sliding a hand into my hair as he slides his other hand into Dominick's, holding our heads side by side. "I love you." His eyes flick between the two of us. "Both of you.

More than I could ever imagine loving one person, let alone two." I watch as he places a gentle kiss on Dominick's mouth. Dom fists Billy's shirt in his hands in aid to draw him closer. I slip around Dom to kneel on the floor. Billy releases Dom and gives my lips the same attention, I grip each of their shirts in my hands to keep myself steady. The love inside of me overwhelms me, bringing tears to my eyes. Billy pulls back and brushes a way tear as Dom drops to kneel along with us. As I look at us all kneeling on the floor, I realise we form a circle. Which is only fitting because although there are three of us, we aren't a love triangle. We're a circle. We're one love made up of three people.

"Mates," Billy breaths the word, and something inside me slides into place. Something I didn't know I was missing.

I gasp. "Is that…?"

"The mate bond?" Dominick finishes, a hand pressed to the centre of his chest.

I close my eyes as I focus on the newness inside me. It's like there's a ball of cord in my centre that has strands leading off it, one hot and one cold. Choosing the hot one, I follow it and find Billy. His love pours out at me. Love for me and Dominick. I can feel everything he is. Even the anxiety of scaring us off with these bonds and how connected they make us. Releasing my grip on his shirt, I blindly reach out for his hand and squeeze it in mine, hoping to show him I'm not scared. Working my way back to the cold strand, I follow it and am not surprised to find Dominick. He's shocked, no doubt doing his own investigating of whatever the bonds feel like inside him. I slip my hand under his shirt and run my fingers over his taut muscles. The cord between us tightens and I realise he must be focusing on me. Opening my eyes, I flick them between the two men I love more than anything in the world, and tell them as much.

"I love you both, more than anything in the world."

Billy's eyes soften.

"I think I'm the luckiest man alive." The emotion in Dominick's voice causes a lump to form in my throat.

Billy stands and reaches a hand out to both of us. "Let's head to bed and I'll show you both exactly how lucky you are." The suggestive wink he throws us says it all. The anxiety pulsing through the room disappears almost immediately and leaves tension in the air, one of need and longing. My men are spectacular. In just a short time I already know they love fiercely, but with Theo's support, we no longer have to hide. Happiness pulses through me.

"First one in bed chooses who bottoms," I shout as I rush past them both, only to be halted by strong arms banding around my waist.

"I'm sorry, sugar, but it ain't gonna be you making that decision." Billy's voice vibrates through his chest against my back, and I laugh, welcoming the sensation of his body against mine.

The air moves around us in a crazy gust. "Are you both forgetting I have vampire speed?" Dominick's laugh carries from somewhere in front of us. Accepting defeat, I turn in Billy's arms as his hold slackens. Sliding my hands to the hem of his shirt, I lift it over his head, pausing to press a kiss to his chest as it comes into view.

If I don't have any control in the bedroom tonight, at least I'll have it getting Billy naked on the way.

11

THE PERFECT GIFT

*W*ith Billy's birthday coming up, I work my way through the local shops hoping to see something that jumps out at me. The idiot didn't want a fuss and only mentioned his birthday two days before the actual event. Dominick left last night pissed at the prospect of trying to throw together a last-minute party. If anyone can do it, Dominick can. The venue is covered because Misty's is the obvious place to do it. That way the vampires and werewolves can be on neutral territory and with my wards, there will be no fights breaking out. I'm not sure how many people know about our relationship… mating. But once we are all in the same room, it's going to be pretty obvious. We can't seem to keep our hands off each other.

We haven't made our mating official before the pack, but Billy seems to think Theo will organise that pack meeting within the next few days. He apparently likes to let the couples get used to the mating bond, which will give it time to settle and will allow the pack to feel it and believe it once we're officially brought before the pack. Although I know Billy is worried about how it will be felt through the pack bonds since both Dominick and I have different supernatural energies to Billy and his pack.

There aren't many stores in town. If I'd have had more

notice, I would have taken a trip to Sydney, but unfortunately, I just don't have the time now. I wander through the last store, running my eyes over the shelves for anything that screams Billy. Spotting a metal sculpture of a person on a motorbike, I pick it up to get a closer look and realise it's actually a wine bottle holder. The bottle slides inside the person's body, and the helmet sits on top of the bottle as if it's the person's head.

"Billy will love that," a female voice says, causing me to jump. I juggle with the sculpture briefly, before placing it back on the shelf and turning to face my company.

"Alyssa…." I stare at the woman who's barely recognizable as the person I knew a few months ago. She looks withdrawn and tired, if the black shadows under her eyes are anything to go by. Alyssa used to always wear pretty summer dresses and had her fiery red hair styled perfectly. Today she's wearing black leggings with what's obviously a guy's T-shirt, and her hair is pulled back into a messy ponytail. "How are ya doing? You're the last person I expected to bump into." Realising it was a stupid question to ask someone who's recently lost her mate, I reach out and pull her into a hug. "It's good to see ya. How did ya know I'm shopping for Billy?" Alyssa hasn't been anywhere near the pack or its members since her mate, Wes, died. I wouldn't have expected her to know about our mating.

She steps back and tugs on her shirt in what looks like a nervous gesture, as she looks down at her feet. "It's his birthday, and seeing what you were looking at, I guessed it had to be for him. That's why I'm shopping today, too." She flicks her eyes up to mine and gives me a small smile. "He's a friend, and although I haven't really been around lately, it doesn't mean I've completely forgotten about the pack and its members. My family."

"Do you have time to grab a coffee? I'd love to catch up

with ya," I offer. Last I heard, Alyssa didn't really leave the house. I'd love to show her she has friends who aren't the packmates she's been hiding from. Friends who can make her feel good and maybe give her a reason to get out of the house more often. Jared, an alpha lion shifter, has been looking after her since she lost her mate. Normally a pack would rally together and look after a lost pack member's mate, but unfortunately, Alyssa couldn't bear to be near another pack member. Feeling their pain at Wes's loss, made her pain all the more overwhelming.

Alyssa checks her watch before glancing around the store. "I… I have the time. It's just… I don't want to risk bumping into anyone else. I'm not ready for that. Especially when Jared isn't around to ground my wolf."

I'd heard at the beginning her wolf had wanted to force her to shift, but because she's pregnant, she can't shift into her wolf form without losing the child. Jared has been using his alpha power to keep her wolf calm. My best friend, Bel, has told me how worried Theo, Alyssa's alpha, is about her losing the child. He thinks the child is the only thing keeping her alive.

Taking Billy's gift off the shelf, I offer Alyssa my arm. "How about grabbing a coffee at my place? It's a two-minute walk away, and there's no chance of seeing any pack members there." I smile, hoping she can see the confidence I have in that statement. I've been living at Billy's lately, so there is no reason for him to turn up at mine. Bel is the only other pack member who may visit me at home, but that doesn't happen without having made plans first.

Seeing Alyssa take a deep and shaky breath, I ready myself for her decline by pulling my arm back. Her small fingers slide into the crook of my elbow before I get it completely away.

"That sounds nice. Thank you." She gives me a small smile, her head tilted, somewhat shyly.

---

*I*t isn't long before we're sitting on my gorgeous rooftop garden, enjoying our mugs of coffee.

Alyssa has her eyes closed, face tilted to the sky. She looks like she's soaking in the sun. "It's amazing up here. Quiet, secluded and freeing." Her voice sounds so much lighter than it had been in the store.

I glance around at the planters full of herbs and veggies —some of them looking a little neglected. "I love this place. It's my little slice of heaven. Although I'll admit, I've been a little distracted lately and not really had the time to enjoy it."

Since I've been staying at Billy's, I haven't had chance to come up here in a while. Even though the thought makes me sad, I don't think it will be changing. Maybe I should think about renting it out or something.

Cradling her mug in her palms, Alyssa swirls the coffee, her eyes on the moving liquid. "Who is this distraction you're talking about?"

"Who... I...," I stumble over my words, not knowing what to say. I don't want to go on about the guys I love when I know her man was torn away from her not long ago.

Alyssa pins me with a determined stare. "Misty, I'm not going to fall apart just because you've fallen in love. I know life goes on, and although everybody felt Wes's loss, their lives didn't stop. Not like mine did."

Leaning forward, I take her hand in mine and give it a gentle squeeze. "I'm sorry about Wes." After letting go of her hand, I sit back in my chair. "Do ya really want to hear about my love life?"

Alyssa places her mug beside her chair on the floor and

places her hands in her lap, before turning her attention on to me. "Yes. Tell me everything."

So, I do. I fill her in on everything that happened between myself, Dominick, and Billy. As I go on in detail, she seems to lose herself in my drama and it's so nice to see a genuine smile on her face.

A phone rings, breaking the spell, and Alyssa reaches into her pocket.

"Hello."

She pauses, listening to whoever is on the other end.

"Jared. I'm fine. I'm having coffee with Misty. I should have called you. I'm sorry. I can come back now." She rambles on, and I can see the sad and heartbroken woman slowly emerging once again. The fact that she was able to smile, even for only a little while, gives me hope that in time she'll have the ability to move on.

"Okay, I'll give you a call when I'm ready to come home."

She gives me a brief smile before thanking Jared and saying goodbye. She slides her phone back into her pocket. "I barely stay out for half an hour, normally. He was worried when I didn't turn up back home."

My stomach grumbles loudly, and I can't help but laugh as I stand. "I guess we should get some lunch. I've got some homemade pumpkin soup in the freezer. There's more than enough for two if you'd like some."

Alyssa picks up her mug and stands too. "I can't say no to pumpkin. It's my favourite." Her smile drops. "It was Wes's too." Her eyes flash from deep brown to ice-blue, which I can only assume to be her wolf's eyes. She lifts her shirt and holds it to her nose, clearly breathing in a scent on the material and baring her baby bump. She locks her brown eyes on mine as she slowly lowers the shirt. "I'm sorry about that. When my sadness hits me hard, my wolf panics. Jared's scent is the only thing that makes her feel safe at the minute. It's why I can't leave the house without wearing his clothes. It's bad enough he has to live with me. I don't want him to feel like he has to spend every minute of the day with me too."

"There's no need to apologise. You do whatever you need to do to get through each day. Jared's an alpha. He was born to look after people. He won't mind in the slightest." I slide my arm over her shoulders and lead her back to my apartment. Having caught sight of Alyssa's bump, my mind starts to wonder what it would be like to carry a child of my own. It's something I've never really considered before. I'd thought I wasn't maternal, but now my heart is fluttering at the idea. Maybe I just needed to be with the right guy—guys. We're currently using protection, but down the line, I think I'd like to have kids.

I flick my eyes from the clock to the sleeping form of Alyssa on the sofa. After having our lunch and chatting some more, we turned on the TV and decided to watch a couple of episodes of *Orange is the New Black*. Alyssa fell asleep around the halfway mark of episode two. I have twenty minutes to get to work. She looks so relaxed, it wouldn't be fair to wake her up. I can't leave her alone in case she wakes up confused about where she is and her wolf gets scared and forces her to change.

Lifting Alyssa's phone off the table, I'm relieved to see there's no lock on it. I scroll through the recent calls and dial Jared.

"Lis, are you ready to be picked up?" he answers.

"Jared, it's Misty."

"Shit. Is Alyssa okay? Her wolf hasn't surfaced, has she?"

A loose strand of hair falls in my face, and I quickly tuck

it behind my ear. "Alyssa's fine. She's asleep on the sofa. The thing is I need to go to work soon, and I don't want to leave her alone."

The sound of keys jingling and a door slamming comes through the phone. "I'm on my way," he says, before disconnecting the call.

After wandering around the apartment tidying up and changing into my work clothes, I'm just pulling my hair back in the mirror near the apartment door when there's a gentle knock. I quickly wind the hair tie around my ponytail one final time, and then I pull open the door.

Stepping back, I give Jared room to enter, and he surprises me by wrapping me up in a hug. "Thanks for looking after Alyssa today. She needs interaction with others. It's just hard getting her to realise that."

I give him a pat on the back before breaking out of his hold. "Alyssa gave me some girl time interaction I didn't even know I needed. It was a great day."

"How was she?"

"Surprised you didn't tell me about Billy's mating." We both turn to find Alyssa leaning against the door frame, her brows raised in question.

"Don't look at me like that. Your wolf is skittish. I wasn't risking upsetting her."

Alyssa walks over to Jared, and he folds her in his arms, clearly anticipating her needs. "I know, and I appreciate it, but please don't keep things from me. I'm feeling stronger every day, and even though I'll never get over losing Wes, I want this baby to survive. I already love it." She steps out of Jared's hold and places a hand on her baby bump. "And I need what's left of Wes to be in the world," she says in a whisper. I can't help wondering whether she meant to say it aloud or not.

I glance at my watch, and my eyes widen at the sight.

"Shoot! I'm going to be late. I've gotta go. You're welcome to stay as long as ya want. Just push the button on the door on your way out."

"Don't keep your customers waiting. Go! I'll grab my things and we'll follow you out. Thanks for today. Jared was right. I needed it." Alyssa doesn't hang around for me to thank her and I don't have time to wait. Grabbing my wallet, phone, and keys, I race out the door, giving Jared a quick wave goodbye on the way past.

12.
GIFT OF THE PAST

BILLY

*S*trong fingers stroking my chest pulls me out of sleep. Grinning, I turn to face Dominick. "Hey," I whisper, not wanting to wake Misty who I can hear snoring gently behind me.

"Hi, handsome." Dom shuffles back to the far side of the bed and I allow him to tug me along with him, knowing the further away from Misty we are, the less chance we have of waking her up. She seemed exhausted earlier and I'd feel bad if we disturbed her sleep. With that thought, I'm suddenly grateful for my extra-big bed.

The fact that Dominick is awake tells me it can't be long since we went to bed, because the sun hasn't risen yet. If it had, Dominick would be a corpse right now.

I frown. "What's wrong?" I ask, peering into his endless black eyes. It's such a shame other people can't feel free to look him in the eye without the risk of falling under his compulsion. They're so beautiful. I could feel down our bond and sense exactly what he's feeling but that would be taking away his privacy, nor is it the reason why mates have bonds. A mate bond is to ensure a couple is always connected. Yes, we have the ability to feel each other's emotions and even get a sense of what they are thinking, but it should only be done if and when the other person allows you to.

65

He lifts a hand and cups my jaw. He moves closer until his lips are a fraction from mine. "I just wanted to kiss you." His lips press against mine in a feather-light kiss.

"As much as I don't mind you kissing me, I know you don't normally sleep until the sun forces you to, but you don't usually wake me up after I've fallen asleep either. So, something is bothering you." I run a finger over his lips.

He presses a kiss to my fingertips. "I just wanted to be the first to wish you happy birthday since I'll miss most of it, while I'm out for the daylight hours." He reaches behind him and picks up a small gift box off the bedside table. The location tells me he must have been up and about before waking me up because it wasn't there before we fell asleep. Dom holds out the perfectly wrapped box and gives me an expectant look.

"I… I told you I don't want a fuss. I—" The look on his face suddenly turns wounded and I force myself to smile. I've hated birthdays for such a long time it's hard to feel different even when I know it will make my mates happier.

"Thank you," I say, as I take the gift and methodically peel away the sticky tape, trying not to think about that one present that started this whole dislike of birthdays, and failing miserably.

The present's wrapped in rainbow-striped paper with a yellow bow on top. I untie the ribbon with one gentle tug and pick the piece of sticky tape across the top and each end.

The paper falls away and the top of the box opens….

I gag.

The blood.

The familiar eyeball staring back at me.

My sister's eyeball.

Dominick's energy runs over my skin as he places his hand on top of my shaking one, bringing me back to the here and now. I lift my eyes to his.

"Here, let me open it for you." He tugs the present out of my hands and I let it go willingly.

I look away as he peels the rest of the sticky tape away, not able to even watch him open it. Ever since I received that awful gift, I've been unable to open a present or even watch someone else do it. It takes me back to that moment where I struggle to pull myself out. I feel the bed shift and hear something hitting the hardwood floor.

"Okay." Dominick places something cold in my hand. "There," he says.

Glancing down, I have no trouble discerning the dog tag necklace in the dark of the room, thanks to my wolf's eyesight. There's a tribal wolf head engraved on the front, and feeling more engraving on the back, I flip it over to find the words *"Love of Three. Wolf of the Three."* As the words register, my heart bursts in my chest. There isn't a better gift he could have given me. This wonderful man is full of surprises. I don't know how people can think he's a heartless monster. He's got the biggest heart I've ever known.

Placing the tag over my head, I hold it to my chest. "It's perfect. Thank you." Sliding my hands over his shoulders, I pull him against me, hooking my leg over his hip before pressing my lips to his. Love rushes through our bond and I don't know if it's me sending it him or him sending it to me, but I don't care. The feel of him getting hard against me sends the blood to my own dick. I rock against him.

Dominick pulls back from the kiss. "This isn't going to get you out of telling me what happened with that present. Tomorrow the three of us will discuss it, okay?"

Reaching down between us, I place my hand around both our erections. "Sure, Dominick. Later. First, let me thank you for my gift properly."

He groans in pleasure before crushing his mouth against

mine in a possessive kiss. His hands slide around the back of my neck, his fingers in a bruising grip.

Feeling the unfamiliar chain around my neck as the cool metal of the dog tag shifts over my chest through my movements, I allow myself to fall into the pleasure my mate offers, our hushed conversation having made the moment feel so intimate. I don't think Dom's gift, no matter how wonderful it was, will take away my fear of gifts, but it has given me a beautiful memory to look back on.

13.
SHOW ME LOVE

MISTY

a hot mouth kisses its way across my shoulder, pulling me to consciousness. "Morning, sunshine." Warm breath blows over my neck, making goosebumps rise across my flesh.

"Mmm… morning, handsome. Shouldn't it be me waking ya up with kisses? It is ya birthday after all."

"I told you, I don't want a fuss." He places a kiss on my neck. "So, it's just like any other day for me—and any other day I'd be ravishing you until you beg me to stop."

Sliding my arm over my shoulder, I tug his head closer towards my jaw as I lean back. "Never. I'd never beg you to stop." I turn enough to claim his mouth with mine.

It doesn't take Billy long to manoeuvre us—having me on my back, and him settled between my legs, ready to claim me with more than just his mouth.

Billy breaks the kiss and I gasp to regain my breath. As he pulls back, a dog tag on a chain brushes against my chest. I've never seen it before.

I lift it up in my hand. "What's this?" I take a closer look at it. "Wolf of the three." The words of the inscription are barely a breath as I say them. I lift my eyes to his. "That's perfect."

"Dom." A smile lights up his face. "He's good at gifts." The love on his face blows me away.

A few months ago, I couldn't even imagine Dom or Billy showing as much love to *anyone*, let alone each other. The fact that they both love me just as much brings tears to my eyes.

He presses a kiss to the tip of my nose. "Hey, don't cry."

"I'm sorry." I wipe the corners of my eyes before the escaping tears run into my ears. "I just can't believe how lucky I am to have you both. Sharing all this love between the three of us is so…" I pause, unable to think of the right word.

"Overwhelming?"

"Yes." I sigh, and tell him the other thing on my mind, since I can feel that I've already ruined the moment—his hardness no longer pressing against me. "His gift is so much better than mine."

Billy rolls us both to our sides so we're face-to-face beside each other. "I'm sure whatever you got me will be wonderful. It's from you, how can it not be?"

I shuffle to the far side of the bed, where Dominick slept last night. Hanging off the bed, I reach underneath and pull out my gift. "It's nothing special. It's more silly than anything. I just saw it and thought of ya." Turning, I find him looking at my terribly wrapped gift with wide eyes. Seeing his face pale, I feel the need to defend the odd-shaped gift. "Alyssa actually said it was perfect for you, so if ya don't like it, you can blame her."

Billy swallows and licks his lips. He looks nervous. *What the hell?* Is this something to do with why he doesn't like to celebrate his birthday? He reaches out with a shaky hand and quickly pulls off the paper. Once the paper is gone so are his nerves. I almost wonder if I imagined things.

"That is so cool. Thank you." He gives me a kiss before having a closer look. He removes the bottle of whisky out of the holder and slides it back in place. "Alyssa was right. It's perfect." He places it gently on the bedside table and turns back to me, a seductive glint in his eye. "Now get your pretty little butt over here so I can thank you properly."

I stare at him, torn between following his request and asking about the fear I'd seen on his face when I pulled out the gift. I'd mistaken it for nervousness at first, but the sudden loss of colour, the shaking hands, it was fear. I can still feel it lingering in our mating bond.

The seductive glint in his eye starts to diminish and in a split second, I'm across the bed and kissing him with all I have. I'll worry about the fear later. Right now, I want to make him forget, and what better way to do it than by climbing into his lap?

"Mmm." He moans into my mouth. "Now this is what I was talking about."

My lips lift at the corners into a grin as he hardens beneath me. "That didn't take long," I say, grinding myself against him.

"Of course, I'm going to be hard within seconds when you're rubbing this warm and wet piece of heaven on me." He reaches a hand between us, teasing a finger over my entrance. Tilting my head back, I close my eyes as the anticipation of him entering me flows over me. "You're sexy as fuck!" His tongue laves my neck before his mouth locks onto it, nipping and sucking, as his fingers work their magic.

Needing more friction, I move in his lap. His thumb flicks at my clitoris, that, combined with the pain/pleasure of his mouth, and I'm suddenly falling apart and at his mercy.

Billy lies back on the bed, pulling me down with him to rest over his chest. I think about moving to take my weight off him, but my jellified limbs are having none of it.

As I just start to think I could maybe move, Billy flips us

over. He pauses, hovering over me, holding his weight up with his arms.

"I love you, more than you could ever know." Billy presses a kiss to my lips.

"Show me, Billy."

He kisses the tip of my nose. "I'm gonna do just that," he says, sliding into me, and we both groan in pleasure.

14

SURPRISE PARTY. NOT

DOMINICK

I materialise in front of Misty's, and the pressure in the air around me changes. The tell-tale sign that someone else is also teleporting into the space.

Ruby appears before me with a quiet pop. Eddie looking pale and ill beside her.

"I'm never doing that again," Eddie says between shallow breaths. "Oh, fuck." He darts around the side of the building, and we hear him heaving.

"Not everyone is made for it, Ruby." I grin, amused by her mate's reaction. It brings back memories of the last time I took someone with me—Gerry. He hates it. He doesn't vomit, but it makes him suffer vertigo until he can sleep it off, which isn't good when you've materialised in the middle of an ambush.

Ruby edges around the corner, obviously wanting to comfort her mate. "He might get used to it."

"Never. Again." Eddie's unfaltering tone comes from around the corner before he appears.

"Feeling better?" Ruby asks, pulling him into a hug.

He shakes his head. "Nausea sucks. It's always better if something comes up, since that usually eases the nauseous feeling."

I laugh. "A drink might settle your stomach."

"It's a free bar. I'll be having more than one." The colour is already coming back to his face, making me think he'll be feeling himself in no time.

"There's no way Misty can afford to put up the free bar. I wonder who's paying for it all?" Ruby muses, and I hold my breath, waiting to see who Eddie will suggest.

"I heard it's the secret mate," Cain says from behind me, causing me to jump. It's not often I'm caught unawares. Being around Billy so much has made me get used to wolf energy that I used to hate so much.

If someone had told me a few years back that I'd not only be dating a wolf but mated to one, I would have laughed in their face. They were good for one thing, and that was the potent blood in their veins.

I'm not as blind as that now. I can see past the enemy species. I can see the good ally they make. More importantly, I feel the love Billy showers me with on a daily basis, and I never want to live without it. The mating bond inside me is such a miraculous thing. I could never have imagined I could feel so connected with someone. Or two someone's in our case. I always thought it would be like a sire bond, but it's nothing like that. Sire bonds are there to keep coven members in line. To ensure the coven is safe and secure. But above all, it's there to ensure the leader is obeyed. The mating bond is a connection of love and respect.

"Don't you know who it is?" Eddie asks, his eyes on Cain, a curious look in his eye.

Cain shakes his head. "I wish I did, but Theo said it's up to them when they break the news." Cain frowns at me. "Anyway, what are you doing here? I thought it was meant to be a private party."

I reach for the door, pulling it open. "Maybe I'm the secret lover," I say as I step inside.

I hear both the guys laughing, and smile. The joke will be

on them in a minute. The three of us discussed and agreed that Billy will make an announcement about our mating once everyone arrives and the doors are locked. Misty's wards are intact and extra strong, thanks to the power Billy and I allowed her to feed into it, so if anyone disagrees with our mating and kicks off, things won't get too out of hand.

"That would explain a lot." I hear Ruby's musing and laugh. At least she's smart enough to think it a possibility.

Billy's face lights up as I walk in the bar. Hearing the guys call out behind me, I can tell they must think it's them he's smiling at. He strides forward, meeting me in the middle of the room. Grabbing the lapels of my jacket, he pulls my body against his, mashing his lips with mine in a crushing kiss.

The bar around us disappears as I slide a hand around the back of his neck, guiding his head where I want him. Opening him up to me, our tongues dance as I grip the shirt at his waist in my hand. I stop myself from ripping it off, remembering where we are and who we're surrounded by.

Breaking the kiss, I rest my forehead against his, giving him time to catch his breath. "I fucking love you," I admit, not caring that anyone in here with supernatural hearing can hear my admission.

"I love you, too." Billy presses a kiss on my lips before stepping back and glancing around the room. "Anyone got an issue with this?" He hooks a thumb between the two of us.

There are shrugs, head shakes, and "No" murmured by many, but surprisingly, there are no arguments about it—or at least no one is admitting them openly.

"Good." Billy nods, happy with the outcome. He gives me one last kiss before pushing me towards the bar. "Go kiss our girl. She's missed you."

15

BEST BIRTHDAY EVER

*G*lancing around the room, I take in the faces of my friends and pack mates, taking note of the few who are giving Dominick shady glances. They know we're mated—they can probably feel him and know why he feels different now they are aware of who he is—so, I don't think any of them would try to hurt him, but I'll remember who doesn't support us, regardless of whether they'd do anything against us or not.

A strong hand pats me on the back. "Wow, I would never have guessed that." I hear the smile behind Cain's words and am grateful for him acting normally with me, even though I'm mated to a guy. Not only a guy, but a vampire.

"He fucking told us as we walked in and neither of us believed it," Eddie admits.

Ruby steps out from under his arm to give me a hug. "Happy birthday, Billy. I know you said no presents but here." She presses an envelope into my hands. "Cain explained the present thing to me. I figured you'd be okay with an envelope. It's from both of us." She gestures between herself and Eddie

Grateful for the consideration, I give her a quick kiss on the forehead before tearing open the envelope and pulling out a gift voucher for a hotel in Sydney. "Thank you." I give her another hug

"Luckily, it's owned by a vampire, so it's safe for Dominick," she says as she steps back.

Pulling Eddie into a man hug, I pat him on the back. "Thanks, buddy."

---

*A*fter I've hugged almost everyone in the bar, I find myself sitting at a booth, glad for the slight reprieve. I feel Bel's energy approach before she comes into view at my side. Her hair looks longer than normal. "Can I join you or are you enjoying the peace too much for company?"

"I'm always happy to have your company, darlin'." I gesture for her to join me. "Your hair looks different."

She slides in opposite me and rolls her eyes as she flicks the long strands over her shoulder. "Selena insisted on straightening it."

I let out a chuckle. "You can't exactly argue with Selena when she gets insisting things."

"It's easier to just let her have her way," she agrees.

I glance over my shoulder, looking for Theo. I find him at the bar chatting with Dominick, who's sitting on a bar stool with Misty on his lap.

Following my eyes, Bel watches Dom and Misty for a second. "You three seem real good together. Misty is happier than I've ever seen her. I'm glad you boys didn't run and hide from her fantasies."

I grin at the thought of that night she let her fantasies slip and am also glad Misty has spoken to Bel about us. The three of us have been pretty inseparable since we got together several weeks ago. I started to worry that Misty hadn't had any girl time. "I love them, more than I could have ever imagined."

Her eye's fall on Theo. "I know exactly what you mean, Billy."

The loved-up look crossing her face has me grinning from ear-to-ear. *Yeah, she knows.*

I settle back in my seat, picking up one of the bottles before me. Even though it's an open bar, everyone seemed to feel the need to bring me a drink when they greeted me, so I'm stuck with half a dozen open beer bottles before me and a couple of glasses of whisky. Bel eyes them up and I push a bottle towards her. "Have one. It's not like I'm going to drink them before they go warm and flat."

"Thanks. Theo was meant to be getting me a drink, but it seems like he's managed to get sidetracked with his conversation over there." Bel swallows a mouthful of the liquid before glancing around the room.

I let my eyes follow hers, seeing pack members dancing and seemingly getting along with the vampires Dominick invited.

"Hey, handsome." Misty climbs into my lap, and I hold her there instead of allowing her to slide across me like she'd intended. "I'm going to deaden ya legs."

I plant a kiss on her temple. "You're as light as a feather." I shuffle across, giving Dom room to sit beside me. He throws his arm over my shoulder, and I settle into his side.

Theo gives Bel's drink a curious glance before placing a cocktail in front of her. "I was sure you thought beer was too gassy."

"It is, but you took too long and I got thirsty." Bel shrugs before downing the bottle and letting out a little belch, before pulling the cocktail towards her.

"Now we're all here...." Bel reaches into her coat and

pulls out a box. It's the size of a ring box, maybe slightly bigger.

My heart beats erratically, making me think it's going to explode out of my chest.

Theo swipes the present off the table and hides it out of sight. "Jesus, Bel. No gifts."

It's too late.

Panic has set in, bringing its friend fear along with it.

My breath coming in sharp gasps. The sound of the bar around me fades out. Black dots float before my eyes, and I'm suddenly aware I'm going to faint, and there's nothing I can do to stop it.

A gentle mouth presses against mine. I close my eyes and breathe in Misty's scent of sage through my nose. My head spins, and I feel like it's too late to recover. The panic and fear are winning this battle. There's nothing for me to do but let it take me under.

Fangs pierce my neck and as Dom draws out my blood, Misty's tongue probes at the seam of my lips, asking for entrance. Arousal flows through me, overpowering all other emotion, and I let Misty in.

All too soon, Dom's fangs retract, and he's licking the wound on my neck. He seems to like doing that even though I have my own ability to heal in a matter of minutes.

Misty pulls back enough to rest our foreheads together.

"Thank you."

"It's what mates do."

I turn to Dom and press a kiss to his lips. "Thank you, too."

"I didn't like what I could feel." He rubs at his chest. "Are you going to tell us who put that fear in you?"

I sigh, not really wanting to relive it all. But my mates deserve to learn the truth. Dom takes my hand in his and gives me the strength to tell them about the worst day of my life.

"It all started when I was a stupid nineteen-year-old." I shake my head, still angry at myself for pissing off a psycho like Luke. Dominick's finger runs over the pulse in my wrist, the repetitive motion calming the anger inside.

"I can tell them if you want?" Theo offers from across the table. Fear and pain crosses Bel's features and immediately I try to calm myself, knowing she's picking up on my emotions. Bel's not only our alpha female, but she's also an empath, which means she picks up on other's emotions. When we lost Wes, the pack's grief took a toll on Bel; she spent days locked away trying to avoid it.

I centre myself, focusing on my mate bond and try to draw what strength I can from my mates in the knowledge that I'll never be truly alone again. "Back then I was in another pack. It wasn't a nice pack like this one. We had some truly unhinged members. One of them—Luke—had a fixation on my twin sister, Tillie, Matilda. I wound him up for well over a year, pissed him off, and his fixation got worse. He started stalking her."

Feeling Misty shaking in my lap, I hug her into me, running my hand up and down her arm, hoping to ease her fear.

"She was terrified of him, and he got off on how much it wound me up. He was older and like I said a complete psycho. I had no chance of winning a fight with him, so there was nothing we could do."

"You did what you could. You did what you thought would help. And normally it would have been enough, if your alpha had been decent. Either of them," Theo says, his voice gruff with anger.

I nod, knowing he's right, but still hating myself for everything I did to end up in that situation in the first place.

"I managed to get the two of us transferred into the Mount Roxby Pack." I lock eyes with Theo as I shake my head, a frown creasing my brow. "I still don't know why your father took us in."

"I don't know why my father did a lot of things," Theo admits, looking about as perplexed at the idea as I feel.

"Anyway, three days after arriving, Tillie went missing." With my anger starting to boil up, I take a calming breath and manage to douse the majority of it. Misty presses a kiss to my cheek, distinguishing the lingering emotion, and I give her a grateful smile.

"We hunted high and low with no luck. Marcus wasn't interested in keeping the search going, and after two days, he ordered us to stop."

"Fucker." Theo slams his fist on the table, causing Bel to jump beside him. He slides a hand over her forearm. "Sorry, sweetheart. The more I hear about the shit he pulled as an alpha, I wish I'd ended him myself."

Bel looks at him with wide eyes. "You didn't?"

"No, Cain challenged him."

Bel's eyes search the room for Cain, and the man in question looks over as if he'd either felt her eyes on him or heard his name, giving her a curious smile but not breaking his conversation with Ruby and Eddie. "I... then why is Cain not the alpha? Do wolf packs work differently to Lion Prides?" Bel asks. Knowing she was brought up in a lion pride and not having any contact with wolves since she was nine, I'm not surprised by her question, and by the adoring look on Theo's face, he isn't either. I'm not even shocked to hear that Theo hasn't told her about how he became alpha. Pack life has been pretty hectic since Bel and Theo mated. It's been one drama after another. I hope we catch a break soon.

"Cain handed the pack to me, but I'll tell you that story

another day." His eyes lock on mine. "Let Billy finish his story first."

"Sorry, Billy, please go on. Tell us what happened to your sister."

Reaching forward, I pat Bel's hand comfortingly, trying to reduce the guilt I can see in her strained face. "It's all good, Bel."

Turning her hand over, she grips mine in hers, giving it a gentle squeeze before releasing it.

"To be honest, I don't know what happened to Tillie. My twenty-first birthday was a week after she went missing and I received a present. I opened it thinking it was something amazing. It wasn't. It... I... I was looking at my sister's eye."

Dominick's fingers grip my shoulder. Feeling down our newly forged mating bond, I feel his anger swelling. Angling myself towards him, I take in the tight lines of his face and the tips of his fangs showing between his teeth as he stares towards Theo.

Theo growls, his wolf clearly not happy with Dom's anger aimed in his direction.

Misty slides off my knee and I move closer to Dom to give her room.

Reaching out, I grip his chin in my hand, forcing him to turn and look at me. "Dom, baby, it was a long time ago. You're kinda pissing Theo's wolf off, and I don't want to have to jump in between a fight with my alpha and my mate."

Dominick closes his eyes, and I watch as his fangs disappear, along with his anger. I stroke my thumb over his lips and he places a kiss on my thumb. "Thank you."

"I'm sorry, Theo."

Theo's head shake catches my attention, and I look back across the table.

"I wasn't growling at you, Dominick." Theo's wolf's eyes

lock on mine. "The fucker who did that to your sister should have been hunted down. I don't care how long it would have taken. My father was a bastard for doing nothing."

My heart breaks a little knowing that if it were a few years later, maybe I would have found my sister alive, and I would never have received that god-awful present.

Dominick's hand squeezes my thigh. "I'm so sorry. If I'd known, I would have given you your gift unwrapped."

"Me too," Misty says as she curls around my bicep. "I'm sorry you lost your sister like that."

I press a kiss to her temple in thanks as the sound of Eddie singing karaoke fills the room. With the love and support of my mates, I know I will always get through these tough times. Not wanting to make this night into something miserable, laden with bad memories, I nudge Dom. "Come on, let's go watch Eddie make a fool out of himself. We are at a party after all."

---

*A*fter hours of karaoke, the party starts to die down, and guests leave at a slow trickle. Cain left early on, needing to be with his mate and their child. I'm not taking it personally. In fact, I don't blame him. It wasn't long ago that he'd been dealing with his own kidnapping nightmare, when the alpha of his daughter's biological father had decided he wanted Olivia in his pack. No, I'm bloody grateful he showed his face at all.

Misty calls out her unlocking charm as Eddie and Ruby walk towards the door, having locked us all in when closing time came and went.

It opens before anyone reaches it, and I glance at Misty, wondering if her spell could have gone wrong. Having heard her use that spell before, I know it means unlock, not open.

The shock in on her face, the slack jaw and wide eyes, tells me it wasn't the spell.

Looking up, I catch sight of Eddie colliding with the female in the doorway. He grabs her by her shoulders to keep her upright.

"Jesus! Are you okay?"

She lifts her blonde head up and looks past Eddie. The eye poking out from behind a fringe locks onto mine. I gasp at the familiarity of her face. The scent that hits me only confirms my suspicions.

I swallow. "Til?" I can barely get the name out.

She's suddenly running at me like a pocket rocket and I move forward a step, letting go of Misty and Dom, not wanting her to knock Misty over trying to get to me.

I open my arms and wrap her in a hug as she collides with me. Breathing her distinctive scent in, I hold her tight. How can this be? I saw her eye. I've spent the last thirteen years thinking she was dead.

Releasing my hold on her, I cradle her head in my hands, lifting her face to look at her. Thanks to the werewolf gene, she hasn't aged much. None of us do, not at the regular pace of humans. It's definitely her. I brush her hair behind her ears, my hand shaking as I see the angry puckered scar over her right eye.

"He sent you it, didn't he?" Her voice wavers, making me think it's a thought she's been wondering for a while.

I nod. "I thought you were dead."

I step away, banging my hands against my head. "How could I have just accepted that as confirmation? What kind of brother does that make me? I should never have stopped looking for you. *Fuck!*" I aim my fists for my head, only to have them stopped by strong hands.

I look into the dark depths of Dominick's eyes. "Listen to me, Billy... anyone would have done the same. Especially when your alpha commanded you to stop looking. You had no fucking choice in the matter." There's no compulsion behind his words, and I know what he's saying is true, but it doesn't mean I have to like it.

Gentle hands tug on my elbow, and I glance down to find Tillie looking at me with sadness in her eye.

"I never imagined he'd do something like that with you alive. I swear," I whisper.

She nods. "I know, Bill."

I run a gentle finger over the puckered white scar, barely touching it but needing to feel it to believe it's real. "It didn't heal." It's not a question, but she answers as if it was.

"No, he used silver thread."

A growl escapes my throat, knowing how much pain that must have caused. Silver is poisonous to werewolves. It burns and impedes our healing abilities. If someone has enough of it in our system, it could kill them, but slowly and painfully.

"Hey. He didn't want me dead."

"No, he just wanted you hurting and me to think you were dead." I struggle to control the growl behind my words.

Tillie places her palm over my heart, and I take a calming breath before asking the question on the tip of my tongue. "How did you get away?"

"He started to forget I was a prisoner and I killed him when the opportunity arose." Her explanation is aggressively to the point, and I recognize that tone. Even though I know there's more to her story, I'm not going to push her to tell me it all now. She'll tell me when she's good and ready.

My heart swells with pride at her surviving for so long, but I also regret that it wasn't me who got to kill him. I pull her into my arms again. "I can't believe I have you back."

Small hands grip around my back, squeezing me tight. "I missed you so much, Billy." The strength of her hold on me tells me she's not malnourished. She doesn't even seem wary about the other people here, who to her are strangers. Not like I'd imagine someone who'd been kidnapped and held captive for so long. She's got a confidence to her that I don't think she ever had, which makes me even more curious about the rest of her story.

"It's good to have you back, Til." I glance down at her, needing to see her reaction for my next question. "You are planning on staying, aren't you?"

"If your alpha will accept me into the pack. We hadn't done the official ceremonies before…."

I glance behind me to where Theo was when Tillie entered, only to find nobody there. A quick flick of my eyes around the room and I find Theo, Bel, Misty, and Dom all sitting at the bar, chatting among themselves.

"What was that between you and the vampire earlier? He wasn't compelling you to stop blaming yourself. It was almost like he was pleading with you. As if he cared."

I look back at Tillie to find her watching Dom, curiosity in her raised brow. "He's my mate."

"A vampire and a wolf?"

I let out a gentle laugh. "No one could be quite as surprised as the two of us." I grab her hand and tug her towards the others. "Come and meet the others."

As we approach, Dom nuzzles at Misty's neck, enticing a giggle out of her that shoots straight to my dick.

"I know he's a vampire, but he looks too cosy with that woman. Let me knock him out," she whispers as we stop beside the four at the bar.

I'm filled with relief to see she hasn't lost her fight.

Dominick is beaming as he looks at us, clearly amused by her comment.

I turn to Tillie. "Til, this is Theo, alpha of the Mount Roxby Pack, and his mate, Bel."

Tillie offers her hand, but Bel jumps up and pulls her into a hug. "It'll be good to have you in the pack, Tillie."

Tillie steps back out of Bel's hold. "I can join the pack?" The uncertainty in her voice tears at my heart.

Theo stands, sliding his arm around Bel's back, tugging her into his side. "Of course, you can, Tillie. You're Billy's sister, you're family."

"Thank you. That's...." She wipes a tear, and I draw her into my side.

"Don't cry, Til. I can't introduce you to my mates when you have puffy red eyes."

She looks up at me wide-eyed. "Mates, as in plural? You have more than one?"

I can't hold back my smirk as I turn to face my mates. "Til, meet my mates, Dom and Misty." I never in my wildest dreams imagined my birthday would turn out like this. That I'd be able to introduce my mates to my twin sister.

Dom kisses her on the hand in the charming way he usually greets the ladies. "It's a pleasure to meet you, Matilda."

"Oh, no. Please don't call me Matilda. It's just Tilda or Tillie."

Misty pushes Dom aside and pulls Tillie into a hug. "Oh, you might have a fight on your hands with Dom. He has a thing against nicknames."

I grip the collar of Dom's shirt, pulling him to bring his lips closer to mine. "I don't know, he seems to have mellowed a lot lately."

"Is that what you think?" Before I can answer him, Dom presses a kiss to my lips.

"Hmm..." I pull back, just enough to look into his endless black eyes. "I love you however I can get you."

"Love suits you, Dom," Theo states, amusement in his voice.

"Theodore Wilson. If you don't shut up—"

I kiss the threat of violence off Dom's lips. Smiling to myself as his hands slide around me, I know he's already forgotten anything Theo was saying.

"Let's take the party back to the pack house," Bel suggests. "We've got more than just a birthday to celebrate now. It's a family reunion." I watch over Dom's shoulder as she glances at Tillie. "That's if you're up to it?"

Tillie nods. "I am. Luke took enough years off me. He's dead now and I'm not going to waste another minute of my life dwelling on him or what he did. Plus, it's my birthday too and I haven't celebrated my birthday in a long time." The conviction behind her words sounds strong, but seeing the shaking of her hands before she folds them across her chest tells me she's not quite come to terms with everything like she wants us to believe. I'll ignore it for now, but I'll be sure to keep my eye on her until we can have some time alone to really chat.

Dom pulls away. "It's not far off dawn so I won't be able to come along, but you should definitely keep the party going."

"We have a safe space for vampires—a blacked-out room, that everyone knows not to enter. You are more than welcome to stay." Theo's offer shocks me enough to have me spinning on the spot to see his face and how genuine his offer is. "What?" he asks, clearly surprised at my reaction.

"Wouldn't your pack feel threatened to have me in the pack house?" Dom asks. Out the corner of my eye, I catch sight of Misty grabbing hold of Dom's hand in hers.

"Dom, you're pack now. You're just as welcome as any other pack member in the pack house."

I'm suddenly assaulted with joy, love, and most of all, gratitude through the mate bond I share with Dom. Theo's words have obviously overwhelmed him to have them affect me so fiercely. "I… thank you, Theo. It means everything to hear you say that. I don't know how I'll ever repay you for this."

Theo steps forward and pats Dom on the arm. "There is nothing to repay. Now, let's go party before you have to die for the day."

Theo and Bel walk arm in arm out the door, and I flick my eyes to my sister as she stands, looking unsure of what to do with herself. Leaving Dom and Misty to each other, I slip my hand into Tillie's.

"Are you ready to meet your new pack, Til?"

"As long as I've got my brother by my side, I'm ready for anything." Hearing the familiar words she used to say when we were younger, reminds me that I actually have my sister back.

Letting go of her hand, I wrap my arm around Tillie's shoulder and kiss the top of her head as we leave the bar. "It's fucking good to have you back, sis."

A small, cold hand slips into my spare one. "Did you enjoy your birthday?" Misty asks.

"I couldn't have wished for anything better." Lifting her hand, I kiss the back of it. "I've two amazing mates who shower me with love I never dreamed I'd be worthy of. And to top it off, I've got my sister back." I squeeze Tillie against my side. "Best birthday ever!"

The End

EXCERPT

Turn the page for an excerpt of **Losing Pride**, *book 5* of the
Mount Roxby series.

Coming in 2019

5.

DISTURBED PRIDE

JARED

Boom. Boom. Boom.

Jumping out of bed, I yank my door open and storm towards the front door, where the banging's coming from. I glance at the clock in the hall and seeing it's only two in the morning. Immediately my annoyance falls away. Nobody would disturb Dad at this time in the night without good reason. Something has to be wrong.

I open the door to find Stephanie, one of the teenagers of the pride, staring at me, eyes wide in terror.

"*Cleaners!* Cleaners are attacking Pete and Rosie's place. Beth told me to come for you… your Dad… I don't."

Seeing her stumbling over her words, I reach out and pull her into a hug. "You did good, Steph."

I hear Dad's thunderous steps behind me.

"What's happening?" Mum voice calls from behind him.

Dad turns. "I told you to wait in the bedroom until I knew it was safe."

I thrust Stephanie towards my mum and dad. "Cleaners are attacking," I say, before running out the door wearing nothing but the sweats I'd slept in.

Saskia falls into step beside me as I reach closer to Pete and Rosie's house. "What the fuck are you doing here?"

"The same thing as you," she mutters, her tone alerting me not to argue with her.

I shouldn't argue anyway. If the Cleaners really are attacking, the more of us that retaliate, the better.

"You take the lead, Jared," Dad whispers, joining us on the path as we reach the top of their long lane-style driveway.

Seeing a slumped figure on the floor, I charge forward, holding my hand behind me and gesturing for Saskia and Dad to stay back. Crouching beside the body, I feel for a pulse. I hear a grumble of pain as I touch him, and the lion's energy pulses against my skin. He rolls onto his back, and I instantly recognise him.

"Simmo, what happened?" I ask, as I gently search his body for injuries, finding at least four bullet holes in the process.

"Jared?" He breathes my name, the pain clear in his barely-there voice. "Cleaners... ran off... gone."

At his words, I wave Dad and Saskia over. "Okay, Simmo. You rest up." I turn to Dad and Saskia. "The Cleaners ran off. They've shot him up good, and he's in a lot of pain."

Saskia crouches beside him, running a gentle hand over his head. "He's burning up." She glances from him to the pair of us with wide eyes, before her blue eyes fall back on him. "Jesus Christ, Simmo. Did they shoot you up with silver?"

Simmo lets out a pained grunt in answer as he tries to curl in on himself.

Roaring, I step forward, ready to charge into the bush after the Cleaners. The fuckers need to die. A hand whips out around my bicep, holding me in place.

"Jared. Don't," Dad orders.

Slowly and deliberately, I turn to face my father. I bite

back my anger at being ordered to stay. Seeing his lion's golden eyes tells me I'm not the only one close to my beast. "The fuckers need to die." I reiterate my thoughts.

Dad releases a sharp breath. "They do." He glances down at Simmo, before looking out to the bush. "It will be pointless following them and stumbling around in the dark. If we leave it until tomorrow, we can follow them right to their base camp and wipe the lot of them out. Not just the couple who attacked here."

Knowing he's right, I take a calming breath, and my lion recedes, liking the thought of taking out as many Cleaners as possible. "I'm going to check in the house. See how the others are doing."

"Good," he says with a nod. "I'll call our healers and tell them to prep the medical rooms."

Striding towards the house, I pick up the scent of blood before I open the doors and know someone is badly hurt. "Hello?" I call. "Pete? Rosie? It's Jared. Are you okay?"

The sound of a relieved sob comes from the back of the house, and I race towards it. Opening a door, I step into the kitchen and am faced with Rosie crouched over Pete's body on the floor. "*Shit!*" I say at the sight, hoping Pete's going to pull through. I don't want to deal with another female losing her mate.

"I'm not as bad as I look. I've told you, darling, most of the blood is David's." Pete lifts a hand and points around the kitchen island. "You might wanna check him out if it's safe. The bastards shot me before I got a good look at him."

"No worries, mate." I round the island in a couple of long strides and lower myself over David's still body, reaching out to search for a pulse. "He's got a pulse. Thank fuck!" I tell Pete, knowing he'll be concerned. Feeling how weak it is under my fingertips, I know he won't survive if the silver stays in any longer.

ALSO BY
AIMIE JENNISON

Mount Roxby Series

Pride to Pack

Forever Young and Beautiful

Reclaiming the One

Rossi Pack Series

Releasing the Wolf

ACKNOWLEDGEMENTS

I want to thank *my family* for supporting me unconditionally. I love you all to pieces.

Sloan from Sloan J designs, I gave you an image and you made me yet another amazing cover. Thank you.

Becky from Hot Tree Editing, you really made me work hard to get this story to be what it is today and I thank you with my whole heart.

My Parabatai, *Sam Destiny*, you are amazing. You inspire me to push myself harder everyday. I'm so glad we got to meet this year and can't wait for the day we'll meet again. Love ya, forever and always.

Finally, to the one who is reading this, Thank YOU. I hope you love my characters and their stories as much as I do.

ABOUT THE AUTHOR

Aimie is a Yorkshire lass calling Queensland, Australia, home. She is a mother to three boys who has always loved to read and write.

Aimie loves to people watch, it's her favourite way to come up with new characters and stories. So next time a stranger is staring at you in the street don't panic, they could be an author basing a character on you.

Aimie would love to hear from you. Comments and questions are always welcome.

For more information:
www.aimiejennison.com
aimiejennison@gmail.com

f facebook.com/AuthorAimieJennison

🐦 twitter.com/Aim4theNeck

📷 instagram.com/aim4theneck

BB bookbub.com/profile/aimie-jennison

g goodreads.com/Aim4theNeck